STEPHEN DAVIS

THE MERLIN DESTINY

CHOSEN TO HELP THE DRAGONS IN
THEIR AGE-OLD BATTLE AGAINST EVIL

STEPHEN DAVIS

THE MERLIN DESTINY

Chosen to help the dragons in their age-old battle against evil

MEREO
Cirencester

Mereo Books

1A The Wool Market Dyer Street Cirencester Gloucestershire GL7 2PR
An imprint of Memoirs Publishing www.mereobooks.com

The Merlin Destiny: 978-1-86151-289-5

First published in Great Britain in 2014
by Mereo Books, an imprint of Memoirs Publishing

A CIP catalogue record for this book is available from the British Library.

Cover design - Ray Lipscombe

The address for Memoirs Publishing Group Limited can be found at www.memoirspublishing.com

The Memoirs Publishing Group Ltd Reg. No. 7834348

The Memoirs Publishing Group supports both The Forest Stewardship Council® (FSC®) and the PEFC® leading international forest-certification organisations. Our books carrying both the FSC label and the PEFC® and are printed on FSC®-certified paper. FSC® is the only forest-certification scheme supported by the leading environmental organisations including Greenpeace. Our paper procurement policy can be found at www.memoirspublishing.com/environment

Typeset in 11/17pt Goudy
by Wiltshire Associates Publisher Services Ltd. Printed and bound in Great Britain by Printondemand-Worldwide, Peterborough PE2 6XD

MIX
Paper from responsible sources
FSC® C004959
PEFC

The sequel to
The Merlin Legacy

CONTENTS

For my lovely wife Phil, Rebecca, Laura, my mother, my sister Deborah, Libby and Sue, and to my nurses and lifetime helpers, Zoe, Leanne, Sarah, and all my amazing nurses - love to you all.

HOW IT ALL BEGAN

This book is the sequel to *The Merlin Legacy*. In the preface of that first book, I told how some years ago, while renovating an old, neglected longhouse in Netherbury, Dorset, I stumbled upon a large, dusty tin box, sealed with some sort of candlewax. When I managed to open it I found it contained a pile of yellowed paper. Upon examination I discovered that I was holding the manuscript of a book, in two volumes. The books proved to be strange, extraordinary and disturbing.

The *The Merlin Legacy* was the first volume. This is the second. There will be no more. Read it and enjoy it; if that is the word.

Stephen Davis, June 2014

THE MERLIN DESTINY

INTRODUCTION

Everything has to start somewhere. If you have read my first account, you will know I have only a limited time in which to put these last memories into some sort of order.

I have set down this second part from memory as faithfully as I can, although if you have read the first account you will have realised that my mind plays the odd trick with chronology, the sequence being in some cases a little confused, sometimes because of forces beyond my control. I beg you to put this down to old age and to make some allowance.

I know, for a reason you will soon learn, that I have just two years to enjoy what life I have. Then, with help, I hope to be united with the love of my life.

If you have read my first account, you will recall how important my predecessor, Jules, was for me when I was a young man. Through him something major arrived in my life and entranced me, and it has become my future.

Horses and hounds still figure prominently in my life, and now and then I will have to stop writing to deal with them. Just now I have an elderly Labrador asleep on my lap. Hardly a lap dog, and when she's awake she natters nineteen to the dozen, until I shove her back on the floor for some peace.

I concluded my last account a few years after my second, shall I say, hospital visit. If you wonder what I mean by that, it's all in the first account; I will not go back over it. In a strange way, although it was a long time ago, it brings on horrible memories which still make me shudder.

I was given no choice with this, shall we say position, and my replacement, a very pleasant young man, had no choice either. I will tell you about him in due course, but he has told me he has no intention of recording his account. With time, the tradition, position, call it what you will, will be forgotten. Its holder will still be there looking after you though.

He came across me the other day and before I could hide my writing, he began to read. I suppose in a way it has helped him to accept what has happened for him. It has filled the blanks in, and after thinking, he agreed that it is important that you, the reader, know a bit of what has looked after you, and generations before.

In an age of gene splicing, space travel and electronic wizardry, there is still a place for the old. This account, my last, will fill a few gaps for you as well. It may be the only record of seven hundred years of witnessing.

CHAPTER 1

A KNIFE IN THE DARK

I had been separating ewes and lambs one late autumn morning and had wandered back home with India, my then current dog, for lunch. Admittedly we were a little late. The leaves were falling off the trees as winter approached, blowing into roadside drifts. The sky was cloud free and there was a hard light, with a fresh wind shoving everything about. It was not really cold, but it was invigorating.

As we came off the hill, India and I mucked around with each other. She would scoot into my feet, muttering and shaking her head. Anyone listening would think it was mock growling, a game, but to me she was talking. She never stopped. I would try to bomb her with a handful of leaves, as with much laughter we wound a way home.

At the farm we had to move in and allow an oil tanker to pass, the driver lifting a hand in thanks, before flipping the gate catch and going into the yard. I walked across, taking the time to stop and ask Fiddlesticks, my new hunter, who was sticking her head over the stable door, how things were. We passed a few moments and then I stopped to kick my wellies off and opened the back door into the kitchen.

I was greeted by my mother's dogs, the warmth and a marvellous smell from fresh baked scones. I heard her voice call 'Hello Peter!' She came round the corner and caught me about to grab a cake.

I couldn't help noticing how bent with age she was getting. She was walking stoically but slowly, and her hair seemed very thin and white. But her eyes still had a wicked smile and her face split into a wide grin as she saw me.

'Oi, get off, not yet! They're still hot, and anyway it will be lunch in a moment,' she said. She looked at me, putting a finger to her lips in a hush sign. Then she beckoned me closer with a finger.

'Zoë is here with her mum,' she whispered. 'They are rather upset. She has had a horrid thing yesterday with her pony. They have been at the police station this morning. Fat lot of good it's done so far.'

'What on earth for? Is she all right?'

She shook her head, shrugging her shoulders and pointing with a bent pastry encrusted finger. 'Well come through, your father's away today as you know, and not back yet, and they'd probably welcome your thoughts. Come on!'

I need to explain that Zoe and her mum Brenda were on their own but managing well, Zoe's dad having run off years ago with his then cleaner. He was only occasionally in touch with them.

'Yes fine, I will' I said, waving an arm for Mother to go first. India and I wandered through the dining room to the TV room, following Mother. We found Zoe and Brenda sitting on the window seat clutching empty coffee cups.

The fire crackled the logs in the hearth, and Mother's terriers looked up at me from their lazy trances in front of it. The two women both looked pale and red-eyed, and Zoë was still crying a little.

'Hello you two, nice to see you. You been having trouble?' I began. It sounded rather pathetic, but what else could I say?

They were both wearing body warmers, and Brenda still had her bobble hat on. Zoë's long brown hair fell down, partly hiding her face. They looked dressed for snow, and the fire did not seem to be touching them at all.

They both looked up, trying to smile a greeting, and then bent down to say hello to India. She put her head on their laps in turn, standing, then a tail wagging.

'Here, give me those empties, don't cuddle them' said Mother gently. 'Go on, tell Peter that horrid story. That is, if you feel you want to' she quickly added. She bent to take the offered cups from them.

'He is always riding over there.' She paused, looking at them and then towards me, giving a 'help me' look.

'I might be able to help somehow' I said, giving a supporting smile. I looked at all three in turn, with Zoë and then her mother looking up at me. My mother caught my eye, and lifted her shoulders in a shrug.

Zoë's mother looked at me, shuffled on her seat and glanced at her daughter.

'Right, I will' she said. 'Zoë is too frightened by the whole thing. The police are coming around again tonight, to tell us all their thoughts and help.' She looked to Zoë, putting a hand on her knee and giving it a squeeze.

It's funny the things that stick in your mind. I had kicked off my wellies by the back door. Socks being hopeless things, they had been drawn down, and lay all wrinkled by my toes. As I pulled a stool over to sit in front of them all, I started pulling my socks up as I talked. Only then did I realise that my right sock had a massive hole and a great white lump of toes and foot were on view. Hoping that this had not been noticed, I pulled my sock back down, covering it, and looked up.

They appeared not to have noticed. Brenda took her daughter's hand and held it. Then she looked at me and began talking.

Zoë often went out on her ancient pony Zebedee for long hacks around the area. Having been on horseback for years she was a safe rider, and her mother was not unduly worried. The summer holidays had seen Zoë riding her new, bigger horse, which her mother had recently bought, nearly every day.

There was, as is the case with many horsy families, a dependable and trusted hairy little pony in the background, an inherited friend who looked after all children. Although this one's legs had now grown rather long, they still made a good pair together, and often could be seen covering many miles.

Zebedee was easily strong enough for this slender girl, and her legs could still just fit the stirrup leathers on their last hole. They had become inseparable, and after many years the little pony knew everything about Zoe. She was a star, and treasured by all.

After tacking up that late afternoon, she had trotted out of the village, then taken a farm track that wound down into a local valley. It was unseasonably warm that day and she had had to wave away a few late flies that pestered her face.

The track gets narrower and great prickly branches of

blackthorn hang down at one point, to be followed by trailing brambles. All this keeps you lying down on your horse's neck. Fortunately on the valley floor the track opens up, to be replaced by boggy ground where a small stream crosses. Zoë and Zeb had begun to wind up the other side of the valley, unintentionally putting up many pheasants as they went; the local farm shoot had release pens running parallel to the track. The birds ran ahead along the track or exploded into the air. An underkeeper saw them and called out, raising a hand in greeting.

The track soon opens up into a muddy farm lane, used by the milkers as they come into the farmyard and parlour from the fields. Zoë had ridden through the yard, and the mechanical noise of the milking clusters could be heard through the open door. The milker, wearing his blue oversuit, saw her pass and lifted a hand before going back to the waiting udders.

The farm track eventually joins a minor road that goes past Lewesdon, and after carefully looking, the pair joined it, heading for the hill. Lewesdon is one of three hills that march across West Dorset, originally used by ancient tribes as hill forts. This one rises to a beech tree crown with two steep sides, gentler to the north. From the top, by moving around a little, one can look across to the sea and the Dorset landscapes.

They trotted along the road, keeping hard in to the left as a few cars came past. The view along here is impressive, with views down across a vale to the distant sea. Today this was a twinkling blue, with far out two vast tankers crawling by along the horizon. A fresh wind played as they trotted along, and the odd glimpse of the sun through the clouds added a little warmth.

Beyond a cottage on the left another farm entrance leads to a path that goes up the hill. This was not exactly a permitted horse path, but they had been sneaking up here for years. The pair had stopped at the base of the hill, Zeb getting the chance to grab a mouthful of grass and try to deal with some blackberries that hung over the bank. Zoë raided her pocket for the chocolate biscuits she had filched from the kitchen tin.

At this point she was not really paying attention to the fact that there were six cars pulled up in the layby at the entrance. She did on reflection realise that it was beginning to get darker, and the temperature had started to drop. She was glad her mother had insisted she pull an old quilted jacket on before going, and almost absent-mindedly, she pulled the collar up.

Gathering the reins together, she set the pony up the hill. The lower slopes did not have a daunting angle, and the track was reasonably wide still. However as they climbed past a fallen beech the track became increasingly narrow and pitted, and increased in gradient. It began to wind its way through clumps of bracken and briars, the surface littered by big lumps of flint.

Zoe shifted her weight forward in the saddle and increased the grip with her knees. The pony bent its head down as it got stuck into getting them both up. Just shy of the flat top the track momentarily levelled out, almost as if for a final rest before the last ascent began. Zoë had got onto this flat and got her pony to halt for a breather. As they stood there, hidden from the top, she realised she could hear strange noises from the top; it sounded like faint singing and beating drums.

The pony lifted its head and pricked its ears, and automatically Zoë patted its neck and spoke reassuringly to it. She was enough of a horsewoman already to know that shying back or rein backing down the slope behind her was potentially dangerous. Fortunately this pony had been virtually bombproof all its life.

She knew enough also to realise that riding at this spot was not allowed in the byelaws, but she had a childish interest in what was happening. She told me later that she wondered if a film company was working, or a TV programme was being made.

She waited and no one appeared, so she pushed the pony on and climbed the last slope to the grassy top.

She found herself on the flanks of a grassy top, dotted with stunted trees. On the farthest edge she could see the beech tree canopy where the trees from the slopes below opened out. She rode on level - and then stopped, horrified by what she could see.

On the far side, a small group of men were dancing around something; a lamb, tied up on the ground. One of the men was covered in a black one-piece gown, but to Zoe's horror the others were stark naked. Their bodies were dripping with what might have been paint. They appeared to have bright blue arms, with slashes of red and yellow. To one side an elderly lady sat beating a drum on her lap, not looking up.

As they danced around, Zoë was horrified to see that one of the men was carrying a long knife, and he was dancing nearer and nearer to the lamb, which twisted its head about and gave out a pathetic bleating. The dancing was getting faster and the singing louder. Suddenly, without any warning, the man with the knife danced in and cut the lamb's throat with a single savage stroke.

At this point Zoë screamed in fear. She pulled her pony's head around quickly as every face turned to her and two of the men started running towards her.

The slope at the top was not pony friendly. Leaning back in the saddle and giving her pony a long rein, Zoe had the presence of mind not to interfere with his mouth or balance. She reached the lower flat just as a voice from up above her shouted 'Stop!'

She did not look back but pushed on. Alternating between a fast walk and a trot, and now and then hugging her ponies neck to avoid being whacked by beech tree switches, she hurried back down the sharp slope, back to the road.

Zoe was petrified, and grateful to be back on the main road, trotting fast towards the farm turn. But within moments she heard cars start, with much reversing and turning. She heard the squeal of brakes and tyres and turned to see that a lorry had come around the corner and one of the turning cars had nearly hit it. But as she watched, one of the other cars pulled away and began accelerating after her.

She turned into the farm track, where the strip of mud up the middle allowed her to canter. To the pony's amazement, he found himself pushed into a gallop. But when she looked back again, the car had turned and followed her.

Zoë hoped desperately that some of the dairymen had seen or heard her coming, but none appeared. She pulled the pony up into a smart trot across the yard, then pushed it back into a canter once back on the farm track. She was pleased to see that the car had stopped at this point, and she saw two farm workers approach it.

Now she pushed the pony on as fast as it could, and sensing her urgency it responded fully. Its head stretched forward as it sucked in air. Its body got lower as it pushed and pushed, with Zoë looking ahead to give it the odd steer, avoiding oncoming ruts. Soon the steep path by the release pens came up, and the pair slowed. Half walking, half trotting, they virtually slid to the valley bottom.

Zoë pulled up by the boggy part and let the pony suck in great breaths. As they stood there she was able to look up the far hill and through the hedge that bordered the road. She could see some of the parked cars go slowly past. She felt her fear return to grip her once again. Why were they so determined to find her? They kept crawling on and went by without stopping, finally disappearing from sight.

Zoë slowly walked the pony up the slope, then scooted unseen across the road onto another path which skirted the village. This track took you through a new planted vineyard, and the edge allowed you to kick on again. Zeb, labouring but still sensing his rider's need for speed, kept going. On reaching the road the pair slowed once again to a trot. A short distance later, they burst breathless into the gates of home.

The pony was very nearly blown. Zoë pushed him into a stable, threw a broken-up bale of straw on the floor, made sure it had a bucket of water and ran off sobbing to tell her mother.

At this point her mother stopped talking for a while and looked at me.

'What did you do then?' I asked her. 'Do you know who they were? What was going on?'

'Well, later I thought we had better tell the police. She was really scared by it all.
Isn't that right Zoë, you were dreadfully frightened by them?. Never mind what they were doing.' She stopped stopping to look up at me.

'What did the police say?'

She told us that an officer had gone up the hill later in the dark and by torchlight he had found the still-warm remains of a fire which had obviously been stamped out. The farm worker could not remember the number of the car, but he did say that the two men in it looked half dressed, and they were extremely rude to him. They had finally driven off at speed after giving him a mouthful of abuse.

The officers had indicated later to the mother that they thought Zoë had interrupted some weird ritual. They did not say, but implied that they thought it was some form of black magic.

This was the point where my mother, with her usual calm brilliance, took over the conversation. She had stressed to them both that they were safe now. Weirdos were about, but it was surely a one-off, and so on.

The humour of the two women did improve, to the point where they had accepted Mother's offer of staying for a bit to eat, sharing our lunch. Later that afternoon I escorted them home by torchlight. Although they lived close enough, it was getting pitch black by then, and we do not have the luxury of street lights.

I saw them both in, helped Zoë check her pony and horse and left them with a cheerful 'night night'. Brenda gave me a kiss and whispered in my ear 'many thanks'. As I left they were waiting for the police to arrive.

'Well what do you make of that?' Mother said as I got back in. I stopped for a moment, struck again by how old and tired she looked. She was staring at me with a vague, far-off look. I went over and for no reason at all, other than that it felt right, I gave her a hug.

'I have no idea, but it sounds like she was lucky to get away. What a bunch of dodgies.'

And then a few months later, the neighbourhood was dealt a terrible blow when a young baby was stolen from its pram in the garden. The local TV stations picked up on this, and soon it became national news. But the police had nothing to report; it seemed nobody had seen anything.

Needless to say the parents and all who knew them were devastated. They appeared on the evening television news, making a plea for information from anyone who might know anything at all about the disappearance of their beloved child. But it all looked as hopeless as it was sad. I remember Mother saying to me in an off-hand way, 'It reminds me of Zoë's story of that group killing the lamb. So many weirdos about these days! All that chanting. Ghastly! I can't bear to think of it.'

She went back to finish her ironing, but for me that was enough, the final push - if I really needed one. Using the excuse of doing a last check of the sheep, I took India and set off up the hill. Although it was now dark, and I was armed only with a dog and a torch, my parents just looked up from their papers and iron, as I left.

'Don't get cold' said mother as we left, shutting the back door.

The lane up the hill was unlit and pitch dark. India rooted about in front and in the beam from the torch I was aware of her stopping and looking back at me every now and then. There were a few stars visible up above through a patchy cloud cover which occasionally parted enough to show a half moon. Although the lane had steep sides below the local fields, it still filled with a cutting wind. On the far side of the valley a tawny owl made its shrieking call.

I began to feel cold and increased my pace. I was still unable to really run, but I could push on a bit. The light of the torch picked up the odd fallen branch, but soon it showed the gate to the top fields.

'I'll wait by the gate' thought India to me. I gave her head a rub and bent down to meet her ear with my nose, rubbing it.

'Fine, stay here, I know how you feel. Won't be long. Listen out for any trouble. I'll call out if you're needed.'

Now at this point, let me say that if you have not read my first account, you will be thinking, yes, I see - talking to a *dog*? Well, I wasn't talking as you would reckon it. It's easier to imagine it as thinking, that's the first thing to explain.

The second thing is that I am not sure why all my dogs through all my years have been uneasy meeting Typos. In fact to be honest, despite me reassuring them, they have all been petrified.

I climbed the gate, not bothering to undo the padlock as my hands were cold. As I walked across the first field, several ewes lifted their heads and ran off. The wind had a cutting edge up here on the hill. Several clouds scudded overhead, blocking now and then the half moon which was trying to shine. On the valley sides two pairs of headlights came slowly down into the village, but apart from three barely visible kitchen lights you would have no indication at all that the village was below us in the night.

The field with our barn still had long grass, which was hopefully being saved until after Christmas. It would not have any use but belly fill for animals, but it all helped.

In front of the barn I paused out of habit to listen and to try and peer through the dark. Although it was highly unlikely that I was not alone, this spot still had a bad memory – a memory of being found out here.

Out of need, and I suppose to be honest still feeling a need for ritual, I lowered myself down using one of the barn uprights. Kneeling down on the cold ground and feeling the wet coming through to my knees, I began reciting the call, the summons, the request - call it what you will.

It in a short time began accelerating on its own, the words gathering speed and volume. It always seems they reach a point when they are unstoppable. My ears began filling with a painful pressure that almost made me cry out.

Just as I felt I had almost had enough, I knew she was there. The air pressure rises, then falls. No animal noises can be heard; all becomes quiet and calm. It's always the same

I opened my eyes and was immediately stunned, amazed and awed all over again. From the first time I saw her, years ago, I have been in love with this amazing thing, this being of wonder.

Typos stood there, rippling the scales along her back. In the moonlight her colour was no more than silver shading to black, although in daylight I knew her leathery coat was a greenish colour, shading to yellow on her legs. Her legs finished in massive sword-like talons. I could even see in the faint light that her shorter front legs were marked by old bloodstains. Her longer and very strong back legs shuffled sideways as she settled, tearing at the turf, peeling it back down to the earth with each movement. She thought to me.

'You called, Myrrdin. You have need?'

She half-opened her massive wings and noisily, with some shaking settled them back down at her sides. I had been told – no, ordered - not to look into her eyes on first meeting, but as before, I did so.

This moment is the most wonderful and powerful joining. It feels as if she is walking around in your head, allowed no secrets, a complete joining. I have repeatedly wondered how I could describe this to you. I cannot; it is beyond words, and glorious.

Her eyes were like deep pools, as big as saucers and jet black. I have over the years seen many emotions rack Typos, but - this may seem even stranger - I always know now when she smiles. She smiled a welcome now. Without any hesitation, it felt natural to grab the barn support and pull myself up. I almost ran over to her, and in a gesture you may wonder at, I threw my arms around her great scaly neck and hugged a welcome.

Her smell is best described as lemony, mixed with leather, but - I have to be honest - her breath, if you catch it, reminds you of an abattoir.

'Yes, I have need' I replied. 'I need your help, or rather we need your help. I will tell you.'

Now I do realise that if you are reading this without having found my first book, you will wonder what is going on. Well, let me say that when I was small Typos' mother, Shola, chose me. I had no choice in this, nor did my predecessor, and incidentally nor has my replacement. Chosen for what, you are possibly thinking. Well… to be Myrrdin, or you may say Merlin.

This is not the stuff of books and films. The character has appeared in various works. This position is ancient, possibly seven hundred or more years. Our duty is really just to be a human witness to certain annual events, but as I have just told you, we can call in times of stress for uniquely powerful help; a dragon.

CHAPTER 2

RETURN OF A DRAGON

'What is it you have need for?' Typos thought to me, and she started scratching behind her right ear with one of her massive talons. If she had been human, she would have been signalling gentle, benign interest, almost sufferance.

I stood away from her, on the edge of the barn, looking up at her.

'A baby has been taken, and no one knows who, why and where it has gone. I know it is not really for you... but I wondered if you could help.'

I hesitated and paused. Typos turned her head on one side, then looked down at me, shifting her posture.

'I can tell you have doubts' she further thought to me. 'What other thing have you not thought?'

Like a numskull, I had forgotten that the mind joining with her was complete. As a younger man it had taken me a few visits from her mother to appreciate this. I swear that Typos smiled and looked down at me, her eyes penetrating.

'Well, well…' I stammered, then began properly. 'A young girl we know had a horrible experience recently, when she saw a group of strange men doing something horrible. They were dancing and prancing around in the dark, and then they killed a lamb.'

I paused, twisting on my feet in embarrassment at the absurdity of the next thing I was going to say.

'They, that is the police suggested perhaps black magic, and now with this baby gone… well my mother worries a lot, you know, probably being daft.' I paused. 'Now I have called you, I realise I have been barmy, I am sorry.'

At this point I shut up, as Typos had drawn herself up to her full height, stretching skywards.

'What is black magic?' she thought to me, settling back down. 'Tell me now.'

I looked up at her, slightly worried at her interest.

'Well, it's a sort of anti-normal religion…' I started to say, but she butted in alarmingly and a small flame appeared at her mouth, splitting the black of the night.

'Is it to bring what you call… devils?' she asked. Her whole attitude had changed. It was as if she was coiling ready for a response.

I stood back further now, frightened by the change in her attitude. 'Well, some would say…' I began and then stopped as I began to remember my trips with her mother. I had watched in horror as she had dealt on many occasions with ghastly apparitions linked to the plague pits above the local villages. The memory shut me up momentarily. 'No it cannot be' was all I could whisper.

'Why do ridiculous humans do this?' she thought to me, now obviously furious. 'Do not go, wait, I look.'

With that she had twitched - gone, disappeared. I did not even get a chance to say any more. As is her wont, she just left. The night seemed blacker, and I realised how cold I was. I was amazed at how her attitude had changed as our meeting had gone on.

Slowly the hill seemed to come back to life, and the tawny owl began calling again across the valley. Further away I heard ewes muttering, and in the valley below a lorry could be heard struggling up the narrow part of the road. Further down the valley, a fox began calling with that strange yelp they use to relocate wandering cubs, and in the hedge behind me the leaves crackled as a stoat hunted.

I was beginning to wonder what on earth Typos was doing when a thought split my head – 'I come!' She appeared at great speed, showers of grass and mud being ripped up by her talons. I flung my arms up to protect my face and eyes.

'I find, get on quick, we will be needed now.'

'What…?' I began to say, but was quiet when I realised her intensity and dominance. Following my injury, or should I say my last injury, I have always had a problem taking up a comfortable position on board. Also I suppose, if looking for excuses, I was getting older.

She almost kneeled down, pushing her great neck forward. I have found that if she does this I can then go alongside and lie backwards over her great wing. In this position I am able to swing my right leg over and then sit up, getting snug between the spines on her neck and wriggling home. Her neck is not too big for me to wrap my legs around it with my feet almost linked below it. Over the years it has become quite snug.

On first riding I had been told to put on sticky overtrousers. My last pair had sadly been destroyed in my last accident with her mother. As I have written already, the memories are bad, and are not for now.

'You ready, I go' was all she thought, following a gentle look back at me.

'Yes fine. Where do we go? What did you find… see?'

Her tone seemed more relaxed, but she was obviously focused on some task.

Now I am afraid that I am going to have to interrupt this account again. To be honest with you, I am starting to doubt the wisdom of hiding these memories in two accounts. I am having to explain a bit.

Let me quickly say that I realise many people are probably very sceptical about the idea of dragons and spirits. The simple fact is that dragons can 'time shift' at will back to any time they wish, but only within their own lifetimes. They cannot go back to a time before their birth, nor go ahead in time to what has yet to happen. Shola told me that in a point in time in the future, brainy scientists will work out this time relativity. I will be long gone by then, but it will happen.

Finally, just so your knowledge is complete, dragon flight is behind us in real time. This is why they are not seen. But occasionally they forget, or circumstances demand their action and they are seen. This is why accounts have appeared through the years about them.

'It took me a time, but I have found the child being taken. It took me many visits, but it is done.'

'Well done. What do we do?' was my limited and hardly adequate response.

'It goes with two men. I go back and we wait' was her reply .

As she twitched the night went, daylight arrived and I knew enough local geography to realise that we were above the address of the child's parents. Below me a modern housing estate spread, rows of small houses, each with a small back garden. Several washing lines carried an odd assortment of clothes, and in one garden an elderly man bent over a few growing bags containing the remains of tomato plants. I shifted my position to look down at a row of parked cars and a small group of boys playing a game of football of sorts in the street with a tennis ball.

'Here is the time and place. Look ahead, over there.'

I strained to look forward as she began to circle. Her wings hardly moved as below me I saw a blue shiny pram in a back garden.

When I think back, this seems on reflection easy in every aspect. The garden had running behind it a small access lane, and as we watched a man knocked on the front door. At the same time, to my horror, another man climbed over the fence into the back garden. Half crouching, he ran to the pram, grabbed the baby and ran back. I wanted to shout out, truly horrified, but of course this was not happening now.

Typos carried on circling as we watched the man, clutching the child to his chest, run to a waiting blue Volvo on a corner. This accelerated away around the block of houses and the other man, who had left the front of the house at a smart walk, got in to another car drove off at a sedate pace out of the village.

The joy of being at height is that your view is marvellous, and with little effort we watched the car leave the village and eventually stop at an old farm down by the river, hardly any distance from where the child had been taken.

'We change time now, to later' thought Typos, and instantly we found ourselves in cloud cover. Now I hope it does not annoy you, but I feel the need to write that with this twitching I felt instantly sick. I could not stop myself. To be honest this seems to be a penalty of the change, and I only feel I should mention it so you know. Sometimes it happens, sometimes not.

Typos circled as I wiped my face.

'I am fine, don't worry' I thought to her.

'You have problem?' she asked. I could not believe she had not been aware. Or was she being polite? But before we could think to each other any more, three cars arrived below us. Two men, one of them carrying a bundle which could have been the baby, came out of the house. They got into the Volvo we had been following and all the cars drove off. It was obvious to us watching up above that they were waiting for other cars to pass before intermittently joining the flowing traffic. They did not want to form a convoy.

Typos followed, now having to work harder. She wanted to keep up with the Volvo, but the wind was stiffer than the day before and our view was obstructed at times by large patches of incoming clouds. All I could do was sit there trying to balance her actions and stay as still as possible. My hands were beginning to chill and I pushed them between my thighs and her neck. This was an action she felt.

'You feel well' was all she thought, craning her head down to watch the car at the same time.

'Perfect, no problem' was all I could think back, not wanting to interrupt.

The car pulled off the main road onto a farm track and I watched a passenger get out and open a gate to let it through. He did not get back in but stayed under a hawthorn on the edge as one by one the other cars turned off. Looking up the lane, he shut the gate and got into the last car. All the cars went across the field and dropped down into a small glade under a stand of beech and ancient oaks.

At this point, 'We go to now' Typos thought to me, and the night returned, but there was hardly a change in the temperature.

'I cannot see, we go down. Do not get off or touch the earth' ordered Typos, perhaps unnecessarily, but I suppose to stress her job.

The ground came up rapidly and as we reached the point where I involuntarily gasped, she fanned her wings and we landed, very gently with no noise at all.

'We will watch' was all she thought. Through the trees I could see the men forming a group around the bundle on the ground, lit by the light from a big fire they had lit.

From the group a faint drumming began growing stronger. As we watched the cloud cover increased. It grew even darker and much colder, and the whole area seemed to be shutting down. The drumming action and then the chanting got stronger, louder and more dominant.

'It begins' she thought to me. 'When I say, you must get off and fetch the infant. Go then with it as best you can. I will find you.'

I did not know what to say. Was I to run in? How could I possibly? As if picking up on my thoughts, she rather reassuringly continued, 'It will work, but this madness begins. Why do you people do this stupidity? You must be quick, be strong for the infant. When you leave me you can be seen by them.'

'Yes, but...'

As I began to think to her, a mist had begun to form around

the group of gyrating men. The drumming and dancing was reaching a new and impossible volume and speed. I felt all Typos' muscles flex, and then a form began to appear in the middle of the group. Indistinct at first, it began to take shape, and sitting where I was on Typos' neck I wanted to hide behind my hands as the ghastly image grew.

It was a two-legged man-like creature, with a hideous head, as tall as two ordinary men. Its arms ended in great hooks, and its legs in great cloven hooves. Its head slowly turned and it pointed at one of the gyrating men, who clutched his abdomen, which opened up. With a kicking scream he fell to the ground, writhed for a time and then was still.

The other men stopped dancing and bowed to the devil-like creature. It had a wolf-like head, with huge red eyes, and as it grinned at the mass around it, hideous teeth showed as it slowly turned its head.

Then among the fog and smoke, one of the men moved forward to pick up the infant on the ground. He half bowing moved across the circle, not looking up, offering his arms forward to the vile creature, which turned to look in our direction and then lower its eyes to the bundle.

'It is now, Get off and go' said Typos. I wrestled my legs over her neck and as I hit the ground, she vanished. I saw faces turn to me and at the same time the monstrous devil creature turned its gaze to me. A force pinned me to the ground and I felt it begin to probe my thoughts. I was rooted to the ground, terrified. The men began to shout and wave their arms about.

Then came a moment I will never forget. Typos, in all her enraged fearsome glory, appeared with a massive ear-splitting roar.

Two of the men on the edge of the group turned to gape at her, their fear obvious. Typos let out an immense roar and discharged a massive blast of flame. They were instantly consumed by fire, and died instantly. Two other men had turned and started to run, but Typos killed them both with a long, flaming gush of fire which caught them and sent them flying through the air burning.

I was horrified to witness this killing. I could not bear it. But at this point the force pinning me down eased and I struggled to my feet. Running across to the man holding the child, I grabbed it and wrested it from his grasp. The creature turned its gaze back to me as Typos put her fiery breath between us. Holding the baby tight to me, I ran and ran.

I caught my right leg a savage blow on a fallen trunk as I ran. Instinctively I held the infant away from me. I felt a pain my leg and the gush of warm blood. I pulled myself up and ran on, until a ditch came up in the dark. I flung myself in and kept as still as I could, clutching the infant's form.

From behind me I heard Typos roar again. I peeped up to look and saw what I took to be the last men staggering about as he too burned to death.

I looked down at the baby, pulling the blankets from its face. It appeared to be sleeping peacefully. It was breathing shallowly but regularly; perhaps it had been drugged with something.

Then there arose a truly ghastly noise, and I peered out to see by the light of the fire Typos involved with a horrific fight with the devilish creature. The pair of them flung each other about, one on top, then the other. The creature clawed at Typos incessantly as she fired bolts of fire at it. Her long talons made contact, and something blue gushed from its belly.

The fight got noisier, and even from the distance I was at, I had to duck away from the odd fiery blast. I was horrified to see the creature yell in triumph as it grabbed at Typos' front leg and snapped it. The noise sounded like a cannon blast. Typos threw her head back and a massive blast of flame split the black night. The branches of the trees overhead caught instantly alight.

The mistake the devil made then was to stop to gloat. As Typos turned she fell on her back, with both the talons on her massive hind legs fully extended and shining. She ripped into the creature's guts. It looked momentarily stunned as it saw its own entrails pouring out. Then it let out a hideous scream, fell to the ground and was still.

I pulled myself out of the ditch, still clutching the baby to me, and shuffled across to the fallen Typos. My leg throbbed badly, but I was horrified to see the state my dragon was in. She sat on her back legs, holding a front leg, which was dripping blood and was bent almost at right angles. It was obviously hideously broken. I looked at her face, and the eye contact we made told me of her pain.

'Come, we must still fight' I thought to her. She got to her back legs, supporting herself with a good front, the useless one dangled loosely, almost swinging to and fro with her movement.

'The child first' I thought to her. 'Can you twitch back? I will look for a moment to replace him. Then your leg, my friend.'

I was trying hard to think how it could be fixed. I could hardly ask a vet. I deliberately did not look around too much, being aware of the smell of burning flesh.

With much manoeuvring, which was painfully real for her, Typos took off and we flew back down to the house.

' You need to alter the time until we have a moment, Typos' I thought. She circled and I saw the view below almost frozen in time. Then came the chance I was waiting for; I saw a policeman push the pram out of the house and leave it for a moment. In the road was parked a white forensics van, presumably for a site meeting. The street lights along the road lit everything up reasonably well, and it was not too dark.

'There Typos, now, go down quick! Our only chance.'

We shot down. She could just fit on the small lawn, although she trampled the border plants and wrecked some of the bushes. 'Do it fast, I must not be seen' her mind snapped at me. I flung myself off, half hopped over to the pram and gently laid the child in. I turned and moved over to Typos' neck, flinging myself on to her. 'Go, I can manage!' I screamed at her, lying over her neck.

She twitched out just as the door opened and began circling a few hundred feet above. The officer came out, and looking down I must admit to a wry smile and laugh as he looked in stunned horror at the crushed grass and flowers. I must then admit to a moment of pure joy, because just then the baby woke. It began waving a leg and crying out for attention.

The cries got the mother running from the house and she seized the child with a gasp of delight. The police officer scratched his head in amazement, then ran out to look up and down the road.

'Come, we are done, my great friend, now we must sort you, somehow,' I said to Typos. She flew us slowly back to the barn, then twitched back to normal time. I half slide and half flung myself onto the ground, wincing with pain as I landed.

'You are hurt?' she enquired, turning her head around to me.

'No, it is nothing.' We came to an abrupt stop and I saw her face. Her eyes were round with pain and stress.

'Lie down' I ordered, taking charge, although I was having to think fast. 'Look, wait here, you are safe, no one will see. I will go and then be back, be brave. Wait.'

As best as I could tried to run across the top field, to the gate which I could just make out in the dark. Painfully slowly it seemed, I got across it to find a waiting India.

'All right?' she though, obviously worried. She was half wagging her tail in obvious concern.

'Nothing serious' I replied.

As we half jogged, half walked at speed down the hill, with me limping along, I told her all.

'What now?' she thought back.

'I don't know, this is ghastly, she has given her all. We must help somehow.'

We reached the yard, and trying to be very quiet, we went into the stable feed room. India told my mother's dogs not to bark and give us away, for fear of their lives. It worked, as there was not a peep from the kitchen.

I raided the horse supplies, taking wads of gamgee, loads of leg bandages, some sachets of painkillers we had for the old horse and a great aerosol of purple spray antibiotic.

Then a brilliant thought came to me. I went through to the feed room and rummaged about until I found a reasonably sharp metal saw. I turned the lights off, and still undiscovered I went through the yard, did the latch as quietly as possible and went back up to Typos.

I thought to her 'we come' and we found her still lying down. As we approached, her head lifted, and I have never seen any animal in such obvious pain.

We had a special relationship then, and I hated seeing her like this. I felt inadequate, and wanted to take her pain away. Somehow and from somewhere, I seemed to take some sort of control. Flinging all my clobber down and moving closer, I looked at her leg. The blood had congealed after forming a large puddle on the floor, visible in the faint moonlight. The skin was broken for a length of possibly two feet. It lay at a peculiar angle below the break, but no bone was showing, only what I took to be red muscle.

All I knew of medicine then was what I had learned from medical dramas on the television, but I had helped our vet when called with the odd horse cut, lambing and that sort. I felt hopeless and out of my depth.

'Your leg has broken, Typos, we must make it straight somehow so it can heal' I thought to her, looking around. It would need strength beyond me, for sure. Maybe I could get the tractor, I started thinking, or perhaps use a car jack.

'I will' she thought, and with a struggle she got up and looked skywards. To my utter amazement, with the claws on her broken leg she grabbed a topmost branch of a tall oak behind us. She closed her wings and fell back, as simple as that. What a logical solution – to use part of a tree.

In the dark of the night the crack sounded horrific, as the tree top gave way, and the hedge she landed on cracked and complained as it flattened.

I fought my way in through the briars and blackthorn around her. She did not move at all, and India charged over. 'It's all right' I reassured her, fighting through the brambles to her side. The broken leg was up in the air, but she did not move at all. The leg looked straight, but it was bleeding heavily.

'Right, all the stuff'. I pointed, struggling out, of the brambles.

Over the next few minutes, with Typos more or less unconscious, I worked. I sprayed the leg wound liberally with purple spray and then used four or five feet of the gamgee, which I held in place with two horse bandages.

Then a moment which to this day I am still rather chuffed about; using the saw, I cut two lengths of the plastic guttering from around the barn. These I then bandaged heavily in place, in the front and then the back of her leg. They made a first-class splint, even if I say it myself.

At this point Typos began to stir.

'Your leg is splinted to hold it in position while the bone mends' I explained, standing near her head. I felt her invade my head, dragging out information, as she struggled to her feet.

'Normally splints stay on for a few weeks' I explained. 'You will not be able to move it. You have to wait for the bones to knit.'

Then I had a horrific thought. 'How will you catch food and eat? You'll starve!' I shook my head in dismay. She could not stay here - I could hardly kill sheep each day for her.

She turned to me. 'This leg feels much safer' she said. 'My daughters will provide'

'Daughters?' I exclaimed, nearly falling over with shock. I had no idea Typos had daughters.

'Yes daughters. I have two. You will never meet, or your next, but the one after will, when I stop.'

She stopped and visibly flinching, moved her front leg. I saw this and had a final thought, although to be honest I was still stunned at what I had heard. I really had not the slightest notion how old she actually was, or really much about her.

'We have painkillers' I said and then, without really thinking, 'What do you think you weigh?'

As I said this I realised what a stupid thing it was to say.

' I mean you are, what... six horses... seven? I would say six possibly.'

'Do you mean can I eat six? Yes, but not now!'

I turned and smiled hugely and went over to my pile of stuff, seeing India in the distance.

'I'm fine... all right' I thought to her, as I pulled six sachets from the strip. Luckily there was an old bucket in the corner of the barn, and somewhat inelegantly Typos licked them out, cleanly, without any comment.

Now the drugs had obviously not been tested on such an animal, but in an emergency - well she could have been a big horse!

It felt inadequate just to say goodbye, so rather hopelessly I thanked her. My words seemed weak, and I gave her neck a big thank-you squeeze. I felt a touch embarrassed as she said she would call me each week. Then she twitched out and went. It is strange what you remember, but as I walked back I realised that my own leg was hurting like hell.

As we walked in, my mother heard the door and excitedly called out, 'They have just found that missing baby! Somebody has put her back, probably the person who stole it. It has just been on the news.'

'That's great' I called back, smiling towards India. 'I'm going to have a soak.'

The local radio reported the boy's miraculous return the next day. It also reported a serious woodland fire which had killed six people, they thought. The fire was so hot that they were unsure how many, or if identification was possible.

Perhaps I should just finish this by saying that Typos and I did meet each week for two months, when I cut off her splint. The leg admittedly was a bit bent but fully functional, and the 'powders' worked so well that she wanted some more – just in case.

CHAPTER 3

MASTER & PUPIL

It has occurred to me that I should spend a moment explaining to you about the next Myrrdin or Merlin, the one to replace me. It began with Jules and Shola all those long years ago. Once she flew me, with Typos tagging along, to show to me the next Merlin chosen by her, as a virtual toddler with his mother.

She had chosen him as the next! You may question… No. I had no say in it. There is no choice; it is all at the behest of the current dragon. That is all I can say.

Incidentally Jules, my predecessor, told me he had been shown me being pushed by my parents, if I remember properly in a go-cart. However, and I suppose luckily for me, this lad's father worked for a local agricultural merchant, and over the years he visited me a few times to fix my old and decrepit tractor. We developed a friendship, to cut a long story short.

In addition he was a fly fisherman, and I think out of sympathy for my physical limitations, he often took me fishing. Then he began to bring his son William along. This lad first watched, then helped and later he had his own rod. In fact, dare I say it, he became rather good at the game, but that is an aside.

Even back then, developing friendships with unrelated children could be fraught with absurd rumours. The way this young man entered my life could on reflection not have been easier. I do not mind admitting that explaining what he was to be eventually, and how he was needed, kept me worried for months, no, years. William will perhaps be gone as well when this account is found, so I can comfortably say that I often thought back to how Jules had got the notion over to me. He waited for the spring 'May spirit', or perhaps if you are from the north you say 'Beltane'.

I got his interest on the banks of the local reservoir, as we stopped fishing to chat. I asked him to think a little about natural forces, nature and the governing forces that control life. It was only light talk at this point, but he was obviously interested, which boosted my confidence.

It was difficult initially as I did not want to appear intrusive or heavy, but I knew I was on a limited time scale, which later I will explain. For whatever reason, he had no choice, like me, in being chosen.

He will hopefully never read this bit, but you can imagine my inner joy when, after we had known each other for a few years, he agreed to meet me one evening to see something special. He was happy and obviously somewhat inquisitive, and in a way I had after all those years become a grandfather figure. I suppose that more to the point, his parents had complete trust in me, rightly so, and I have never exposed him to any risk.

From all those years ago, helping me to recapture my yearly rituals, Typos had been flying me to the valley edge above our village. I, or shall I now say we, have to witness a spring ceremony, and this Typos had been taking me to.

Now you may accuse me of being chicken, but I thought at the time that introducing that concept to my replacement was at that point possibly too much. We needed therefore to walk to the scene.

I have realised that finally, for the moment, I need to spell out to you that to avoid too much detective work, I have as in my last account changed some names. The job they do, and will carry on doing, is too important.

It was a warm, barmy evening as William set out with me along the lane out of the village. It's a typical narrow West Dorset lane, with the odd passing place hacked into the edges for cars. The banks were growing high with cow parsley, dandelions and milk thistles and the hedges swung in the odd breeze, the new growth untrimmed as yet by the flails of the Council. It was easy to locate the new birds' nests as the parents slipped out to get food to satisfy their insatiable, gaping nestlings.

As we walked up the steep part, we stopped, turned and looked back on the village below. The rookery was busy in the closing light, with much cawing and squabbling from the now well-developed youngsters. On the far side the view was split by the setting sun, a burning red disc, defying you to look at it.

At the top of the rise the lane joins one of the main roads, and with great care we crossed between the traffic and started up the long, slow climb opposite. The track on the lower slopes is a slog, but it is just grass and easy enough. It passes through lumps of bracken, past the odd bank of brambles and through some large stands of beech trees,

We made small talk between breaths, inconsequential and unmemorable, until we finally stopped at the top. Breathless, we looked upon a superb view.

I often used to come up here on a horse – I still do - stopping to take in the view. Now that I am old, with an old horse and an even older hound, this view refreshes me. This probably sounds strange to you, until you see it.

To thc south the sea was twinkling in the setting sunlight and distant boats could just be seen, moored to fish or moving on. To the west the sun seemed to be crashing into the beech-clad Lewesdon hill, and Pilsdon Hill beyond that was already a dark lump. The far rise of the valley hid all but a small part of the country to the north, and behind us, to the east, a fraction of the hill still rising was our route.

A soft, warm wind tugged at our clothes and hair, bringing smells of soil, hay and vegetation. As we carried on, I was a little worried by the time. It was already hinting at darkness and I had underestimated the distance. Spoilt by being flown, I suppose.

The ground levels out at the top, and we climbed over a gate which was tied up and held together with string. We went around the margin of a new wheat crop, walking in the rough, weedy edge. Rejoining a small lane, we increased our pace until we turned off in front of the manor house. A small track begins here and I stopped, turned to William and then pointed down the hill, along the bracken edge.

'We are going down here' I said. 'We're heading to that valley you can just see marked by that line of trees.' I looked down at his feet. 'It's not muddy, don't worry' I added, looking back up at him and smiling.

Whatever the weather, Will always seemed to be stuck in old trainers, truly filthy but much-loved shorts and invariably a great big baggy jumper. He smiled back at me, his eyes looking inquisitive.

'Yes, but what then? What are we going to see?'

On reflection I was perhaps a bit uninformative at this point, remembering my own thoughts the first time.

'Look it is tricky, it is special for you' I said, turning around to look at him. 'It is unique for you, as it was for me. I will explain it all as we go back, I promise, but you have to trust me. I was shown this years ago, as I am about to show you now, and have seen it now for many years. It is always truly wonderful. Come on, it'll be fine.' I turned to walk on. I know at this point that I expected him to stop, but he carried on following me.

The track at this point gives way into a muddy bridleway, and then at the bottom we turned off. 'We'll go around that boggy bit and up the far side' I half-whispered. He nodded back, and I turned and set off.

I led him around the sticky mud and then up the far side, which is capped by odd stunted bushes which are mainly holly and hawthorn. At the top, a small flat valley below could be seen in the failing light. Dotted with bramble patches, it runs from west to east.

In the virtual dark I pointed to a small leaf-filled depression under a big holly to one side. Bending low, I worked my way in, beckoning him to follow. We both settled down, without saying anything, looking across the valley floor.

The woods around us were now dark and filled with nature's sounds. We both jumped as above us it seemed a pigeon crash-landed, with a great noise of fluttering leaves. Pheasants gave territorial calls, the dogs in the far-off manor could be heard barking, and then nearer two tawny owls began swearing at each other.

William turned his head to me and I saw his teeth flash as he smiled, but then he spun his head back as below us to the west a bell-like noise sounded. I have seen what happens next many times now, and I have to say it has always entranced me.

The music, if you can call it that, grew in volume. It was predominantly the sound of bells, magical and harmonious, and it was as always accompanied by an increasing blue light which grew in intensity. The light filled the valley below, and it seemed to be centred on a figure in the middle who now appeared below us.

I heard an intake of breath from William and was aware of him half rising as if for a better look. I reached for his jacket and pulled him back down. He turned to look at me and I put a finger to my lips. He nodded and turned to look.

The figure below us had now appeared clearly. She was a breathtaking, achingly beautiful woman. As she walked serenely along she was taking things from a basket she carried. Still, after all these years, I do not know what they are. I have never seen or heard them land on the ground.

She wore a long trailing gown, fastened at the waist by a big leather belt. Her long blonde hair was wonderful, flying behind her as if tormented by a gale. She had a wondrous escort, initially that night of three deer which walked behind her and occasionally ran off in front. Soon there followed four foxes, running to and fro, in front then back to her feet.

Finally two badgers appeared, their masks very obvious in the light as they sniffed and snorted in front of her.

When she drew level with us, she stopped and slowly turned her head to look up. Two of the foxes had run back and leaving her feet, ran halfway up the bank towards us. Both whimpered, put their brushes between their legs and almost on their bellies, crawled back to her. She bent down towards them, and must have said something, lost to us. Both virtually bounded up into the air and then ran on.

The lady turned her head again to us, and I felt immense power from her eyes. In all my years of seeing her there has been no conversation, no words; her look is enough.

I took my new Merlin's hand as years ago Jules had taken mine, and lifted it for her to see. She did not nod her head or give any acknowledgement, but looked intently at each of us in turn. I lowered William's hand as she turned back on track, her arm swinging again, continue to scatter the mysterious provender. The light dimmed and the musical noise faded and finally stopped.

'What… what was that all about?' asked William. I smiled as he blurted out the same questions I had asked of Jules years before.

'Don't worry' I told him. 'As we walk back I will try to explain it all. Suffice it to say you are one of only a few in this island who see her.'

I stopped talking for a moment, as it was hard to see where my feet were going in the dark. My eyes are now pretty poor, and even then, last year, they were hopeless without good light.

'Later in the year I will take you to meet the other watchers' I told him. I turned to see if that term produced a reaction. 'They do the same job and have similar honour in every country.'

I paused, letting this sink in.

'You are now part of an ancient and venerated position. To be honest you, like me, were chosen to do this when you were tiny. Don't worry now, soon all will make sense.'

We carried on walking. I was concentrating on the track, so we did not natter. On reaching the road, before turning off for the hill top, we carried on. Gently, and trying to put it simply, I explained it as I remembered as Jules had to me.

You will need to find my first account to follow this, but shall I say that I began a process of description which I expanded on over the minutes that followed.

'The first running animals have been called her forwarders. Jules has told me that he became convinced that she does not really recognise modern roads. The animals run first, making sure it is safe.' In fact I knew this was the truth as Milly, my old wolfhound, had confirmed it to me years before.

I paused and then said 'Like me, you have seen the odd road casualty, the odd squashed fox. Well for sure there are accidents but…' I stopped as the enormity of this came back to me. 'At this time of year they give their lives for her, making sure she can go ahead safely.'

I stopped again, then looked at him, making him look at me.

'Without her nature will not properly wake. She is vital for all new life. With so much pressure from man now on the environment, well...'

I did not want to get heavy at that point, being worried how he would deal with it all. He had been chosen, I explained, to carry on a vital role, the witnessing of a key ritual, a process that ensured that the land came successfully out of its winter sleep. I did not want to frighten him any more for now. I gently added that the forces that govern the water had to be acknowledged too. Later in the year we would do this, together.

I was about to mention the wind forces, but now bad memories returned. It was really Typos who had this problem anyway. I did not feel that getting into heavy descriptions of the significance of his position was necessary at this point. It worried me immensely though that I had so little time to tell him all.

Then I mentioned it; the one thing that must have caused Jules so much worry as well. I stopped walking and turned to look him in the eye, very aware of him tuning momentarily away, embarrassed.

'In a few weeks' time you will meet Typos' I said. 'She wants to meet you, and in a way she helped to choose you.'

'Who is Typos?'

'I am not really able to explain, but don't worry, she will introduce herself. She is large, but she is kind and gentle.' I nearly added - as long as you are on the right side.

We walked back through the night, now helped by a full moon, and William fired questions at me. It had become colder now, and the air was laden with the smells of new growth. Bats wheeled overhead in the dark, black shapes whipping about under the scudding clouds. I tried gently to explain that although science answered and had dealt with many things, there was much more to know. Humans were in a way incidental to the forces that regulated things like natural growth, the seasons, water and wind. Over the next year I would show and explain more to him. The spring queen he had seen tonight was just the start; there was much to follow. He would not be entirely alone, and Typos would help him, but like me his life would be changed.

At this point I stopped and paused. 'I have never married or had children, let me say right away,' I said. I looked across at him and he looked up, obviously embarrassed again.

'Let me quickly say that I have had lots of lady friends, and to be honest one waits for me now... when I am finished.' I paused. 'In fact one who is rather special, but this life that you are now in has too many unknowns, and children just do not fit.' I stopped again, and he looked at me.

'But I will still need college and a job, surely? I have got to earn a living, got to eat, live somewhere!'

'Of course' I smiled, 'but you will have an immense plus on your side, have no fear of that, a big asset!'

Soon we were back at his scooter, and I stood back smiling as he wrestled his crash helmet on.

'That'll give you something to keep you awake,' I joked. 'You won't sleep. Look, I know you didn't ask for it, even expect it. I didn't choose you, but you are chosen. You must not tell anyone ever, by the way, or goodness knows what will happen. I cannot stress that enough. Keep it to yourself. Go on, ride carefully, have a good kip and come and see me here in two weeks. You can meet Typos then. You will like her.'

He turned his lights on, waved a goodbye and the scooter whined off, leaving me to wander home.

That was last year, and now I will just add a final thought for you at this point. In my first account you will come across an account of Jules' last visit to this white queen, shall I call her, at Beltane. You will find that I was then at a loss to know why he was so upset and why as we walked back in the dark he was tearful. Well this year, in fact just a few weeks ago, was definitely my last time.

How do I know? Well, my years are used up. I was a bit, well more than a bit, emotional, to be honest with you, and William was worried. It was impossible for me to tell him that I had seen Typos for the last time. I always wondered why Jules had not told me he was going, and now I know. I can hardly tell William that soon he will be all alone, except for Typos of course.

Was I sad? To be honest, yes. It's dreadful to know that part of your life, a very special part, will stop. However, as I hinted at the start of these memoirs, Typos has my future in hand. I have no fear, but be brave for me.

Now enough of this. I will move on, but I still have lots I want to tell you, and I desperately do not want to appear maudlin.

CHAPTER 4

WILLIAM MEETS TYPOS

This was the moment I feared most, the first meeting.

I had arranged with William that he would come over to me after his college day had finished, and right on cue I heard the whine of his scooter in the yard. I carried on writing, just to finish an early bit from my memory and not wanting to stop at that moment.

William was greeted by an avalanche of dogs. There was much joshing and ear rubbing from him, and much tail-wagging from my three dogs.

'I won't be a mo,' I called out through the open kitchen door, looking to see my visitor. He was a tall, skinny lad, with arms that looked almost skeletal. The puberty growth spurt had stripped any fat off him, and each time I saw him he had changed; taller, broader and I have to say, more gangly. His long fair hair hung all around his face, always so long it nearly needed a plait. An old bomber jacket above torn jeans completed the vision, and under his arm he carried a scratched jet-black crash helmet. Today his usual shorts had been replaced by a pair of old jeans, but his feet wore the usual trainers.

'Stick the kettle on, we've got time for a quickie before she comes,' I shouted through. He looked up and smiled, pushing dogs out of the way and walking in.

'Got any bickies?' he called. 'I'm starving. I could eat a horse.'

'Tin is on the side, help yourself,' I called back, smiling to myself. Why are young men always hungry? I remember I was.

I finished writing and walked through to the kitchen, where I found him fishing teabags out of two mugs, surrounded by a circle of adoring dogs.

'The dogs will be fed in about an hour, don't give them anything, they'll get fat,' I said. He looked sheepishly at me. 'Just a broken bit, only a morsel, don't worry', he said, and turned to fiddle with the mugs.

I smiled as India thought to me 'It was only a bit, we will have less dinner, don't worry'. Hopelessly outnumbered and inwardly pleased that he got on so well with them, I led him into the garden trying to sip boiling tea and chomping digestives.

'We'll have to go up the hill for Typos, she needs, shall I say, a bit of room to get in' I said.

'She's not flying in then?' He bent down to grab a ball for the dogs and throw it.

'Well… actually, yes she is' I answered, trying not to look at him, wondering how I could explain things.

'What, a plane? It's too small up there surely? Her own helicopter, eh? Can we get a go, have you flown with her?'

He paused, stopping and looking intently at me.

'Well I have flown with her a lot, possibly for the last… well, fifty years.'

He butted in 'Fifty years? She must be ancient. Don't they have age limits or that sort of thing?'

'No don't worry It's a bit different, you'll see. She is lovely, very kind, old yes, but you would never know, she doesn't look it.' I paused, thinking to myself, 'just you wait!'

After having fed and settled the dogs, we set off up the lane to the top fields. India knew what was happening and although she offered to come along, she was relieved when I reassured her that we would be all right. As I have said before, I have never had a dog that liked meeting Typos, they are all frightened silly of her.

The way up is a bit of a push for an old wreck like me, and we ambled along, just nattering. We had not gone more than a hundred yards up the hill when we met an elderly couple coming down. Jim and Eileen had lived in the village as long as I had, and I often stopped to natter to them. Their old retriever wagged a meeting and I thought a greeting to her, passing inconsequential thoughts.

'You know Peter, sometimes I think you have nicked that dog' said Jim. 'You have always been so accepted, it's strange.' He paused, grinning to his wife. 'Nice to see though.'

I laughed back, and after saying 'be safe' and 'cheerio', we walked on.

In fact that ancient dog and I had had many conversations. She loved her owners but really had always wanted to work, and felt underused.

William and I reached the top, and after wrestling with the hasp, I stopped to check my sheep.

'Surely we've got to get a move on' he said, glancing around at the sky. He looked at me counting sheep. I walked up to look more closely at one ewe which was limping a little.

'That's all right. We have to go over to that barn, the one on the far side.' I pointed to the far hedge as I walked back to him. 'Look William, just one thing. Typos is a bit sensitive about her eyes. It's not a big deal, but try not to stare at them, well at least until I say.'

I looked at him and smiled.

'What's wrong with them… has she got a wonky eye, or a false one?'

'No, nothing like that. 'Just respect her. No big problem, I promise.'

We walked on across the field, watching a hovering kestrel which was mousing on the valley edge. The view up here is wonderful. Looking down into Netherbury we saw two lorries working their way through, laden with last season's hay. On the far side cows grazed, and from the village we could hear children playing. A cold wind rolled in, gusting under scudding clouds. The upper winds were fairly strong, heading inland laden with moisture from the sea they had just crossed.

I had been wondering how on earth I would get Typos introduced, still remembering my own abject fear.

'Right. Look William I will call her now. Go and sit on that old bale of hay in the corner. You'll need to trust me fully.'

I looked at him, trying to show calm but absolute control to reassure him.

'Yes, don't worry, I trust you, but frankly she sounds like… with respect, an old dear. Nice, I'm sure' he added. 'So I'm not worried. But I don't see a radio or anything – how are you going to call her?'

'Well she is not quite an elderly lady… but just for you, your future, your position…' I stopped, as he looked a bit puzzled.

'Right, as I promised, I'll call her. She's lovely, but let's say she's unusual. Now stay put. I don't need a radio, I'll do it now. Just watch.'

I knelt down, using the barn stanchion to lower myself, and looked across at William, giving him a smile before shutting my eyes. I can remember thinking 'My word, here we go, now or never.

This time I said the chant, or call, out loud. I can remember thinking that this was going to blow his calm confidence away. The chant is repetitive; it involves a series of reverential phrase being repeated as you face the north west, almost like chants in high Roman Catholic services. After a few repetitions it gathers its own momentum, gathering energy and pace. It almost says itself, filling your head, until you lose control. I felt the usual pressure rise, which is momentarily immense, almost forcing you to the ground, with your ears about to burst. All then goes deathly quiet; no sheep can be heard, no birds sing. I knew she was there when I heard her tail slicing at the grass.

I opened my eyes, and there she was in front of me.

Today she was holding herself at full height, almost stretching, with her wings initially outstretched, and then with a great forward and back shake she pulled them into her sides. Settling, she bent down to look at me.

'Myrrdin, you have need, you call?'

Her great black saucer-like eyes held me, and we joined as only we can. It is almost as if she is walking around in your head, a complete invasion. I was almost overcome. Laughing with joy, I struggled to my feet and went over to throw my arms around her scaly neck. This probably sounds weird, perverse, perhaps worrying, but after all this dragon and I have endured it just felt right.

In simple terms she is big, as big, I suppose, as a London bus. She has a great big square head on a long neck, which carries increasing size scales and thorny spikes from the top of her neck, which get bigger as they move down her body. Her front legs are carried by shoulder blades which heave massively as she moves. Her large and obviously strong back legs were coiled under her. Those terrifying talons were noticeably bloodstained and jammed into those of her back right leg were lumps of wool.

As to the smell – definitely lemony, and a little leathery. I cannot describe it better than that.

'As we have discussed, tonight the new Myrrdin you chose with your mother is here to meet you' I thought.

'Where?' she responded.

I turned round. There was no sign of William.

'He went as I twitched, down the hill now' Typos thought to me. She almost seemed to be grinning.

'Blast, no!' I said out loud. 'I didn't want it to go like this at all.' I looked around her bulk down the hill and glimpsed the top of William's head. He was hiding in a ditch at the hill base.

'Wait, just wait' I said to Typos as I started to the hedge.

'I will, just call.' She twitched out.

Half running and half walking, moving as best I could, I tried to go down the fence line, and getting to the tied-up gate, I started to climb it.

'William, William! It's all right, hang on a mo. I am coming. Wait!'

Once over the gate I started down the hill, desperately wondering what on earth to do. Dragons are a bad concept for many and I supposed that in all her frightening glory, her sudden appearance was too much. They are the stuff of fairy stories, after all.

I did think back to my first encounter with Shola, and how she had flown slowly in. That had been scary enough, but we were on a hill top then, a long way from watching eyes.

I reached the ditch and spotted the back of William's bomber jacket. I stopped walking and gently called to him, trying to keep my voice level, although I was gasping for breath from running.

'Look William, it's all right, I promise' I urged him. 'You should have seen me when I saw her mother first time. I was a gibbering wreck. Look, I'm sorry, but well… there is no easy way to explain this, is there?'

I stopped, letting what I was saying sink in.

'Typos is a dragon, yes. She's only for you, no one else. I have been with her for years now. This is not an easy thought, but you have been chosen to witness for all humans her deeds.'

I stopped and then said in a firmer tone, 'You are unique, yes. There are other watchers for the May Queen moving and you will meet them. But just for you are the water forces. And you will go with Typos to witness the Wind Furies.'

I stopped, seeing the jacket move, and William looked up at me. His face was deathly white and I was mortified to see that his eyes were red. He looked utterly shocked, and I do not mind admitting that I felt guilty.

'I'm sorry, it perhaps is not easy, perhaps ghastly first of all to think it, but you have been chosen. You will replace me. You will carry on the line.'

I stopped and reached out offering my hand to pull him out of the ditch. His knees were soaked and he shivered a little.

'Come on Will, jump a bit, swing your arms, go on' I urged him, and he began, looking at me with a face that spoke of fear but at the same time was full of questions.

'Where has she gone?' He managed at last to say.

'Well, she waits for you, it is a simple as that.'

He stopped jumping and began fishing in a pocket, producing a revolting grey handkerchief, which he blew noisily into.

'Where?' he looked quickly around, almost ducking down. I lifted a hand, smiling. 'It's not like that. It is easier than you could ever think for her. Look, come and lean on that gate for a moment. Even if you don't need to, I do! I am much older than you and chasing after you has made me rather tired.'

I do remember feeling actually pleased as he smiled. He was still looking around and back up the hill furtively, but he did walk over with me. Leaning on the gate once again, I thought I was probably better telling all and facing the results. With him clinging to every word and not asking any questions at all, I began.

'Right, listen,' I said, taking his shoulders with my hands and looking straight at him. 'As I said before, you are like me, and one day when you are much older you will be saying the same to your replacement.' At this point I definitely did not feel able to tell him that when he was eighty five his life would stop, whatever happened.

'Like me, when I am gone, you will be the new Merlin, keeping it going on and on. I will show you many things, many strange things, just for you. The watchers you know about have seen the May or Beltane ritual watching. Now as a perk of the job you have Typos as a mate, but you have to help her as well. You will learn how to call, summon her, just for your need, as you saw me do. Just imagine all your life coming up with her as a friend! A helper! The things you will see…'

'But she has gone now' he butted in.

'No, not really gone.' I paused, wondering how to explain the next part.

'This is easy to think of. Dragons can manipulate time. No, hang on a minute…' I lifted a hand, as he was about to say something. 'This is slightly harder to get a grip on, but they are normally just a bit behind us in time. That's why unless they forget or get it wrong they are not seen, or well - only now and then. I have learned that they cannot go forward and they can only back as far as their birth.'

It did not feel at all right then to explain how Typos' mother had often taken me back to centuries before, or to go into long explanations of how we always had to stay on her.

'Also, you need to know that they do not really talk, that is out aloud, but in your head. Don't worry, she will explain. Now listen, she is waiting for me to call.'

'Where is she?' yelled William, looking around and inadvertently grabbing me.

'No, look don't worry, stay with me. Let's go back up to the barn. It's a bit on view here. Come on.'

With that we slowly walked up the hill, William trailing behind. In the barn I stood behind him firmly holding his shoulders and facing out to the field.

'Right, now I have got you safe, I am going to give her a shout,' I half joked, giving his shoulders a squeeze. He did not say anything at all, but I felt him tense as if preparing to run.

'All ready?' I asked.

'Yes, but do not dare let go, please, please!'

'I won't. Now, she comes.'

With her usual ear-popping blast of pressure, Typos appeared in front of us, lying down and turned away, her tail twitching slowly from side to side. Her head and neck lay flat on the ground in front of her. William took her in, and I did feel him relax a little as I pointed out her magnificent shape and strength, her folded wings and the great talons just visible on one side.

'Come on, we will go around to her head so she can see you properly.' Holding his hand, half tugging and with a bit of cajoling, I got him to walk to the front. Typos' eyes were tight shut and hidden by her great soft eyelashes. It may sound odd, perverse even, but I do not mind admitting how fond I felt of her.

'We are complete, Typos' I thought to her. 'This is my replacement, the new Myrrdin, to help you.'

She opened her eyes, and that amazing, wonderful joining took place with William, her new Merlin. She lifted her head a little to his head height.

I walked away at this point feeling as if I was unnecessary, my job done. I turned when a few yards away to look back at a once young man, a mere boy, changed into one of the most privileged people on earth.

He like me, had no choice. He was not asked, and now his life was out of his control. He was the latest chapter in an ancient lineage, and one day he would be watching his replacement.

The two of them stayed locked in a mental union for possibly ten minutes, then Typos turned her head to me.

'Well I go, until there is need,' she said, and with that she twitched out of our presence, with just a last look at me, one hinting at a smile. I looked at William, more relaxed and now almost sleepy.

'Come on, I think a big mug of tea before you go back young

man. Ask me everything on your mind as we go back.' I gave him a fatherly hug. 'Making more sense now?'

'Yes, but boy I have got a headache!' he said, shaking and then clutching his head.

'It is only the first few times,' I smiled and repeated myself as we headed home.

Now I am going to interrupt this thread to tell you about another dragon link, one which is just as important and equally ancient.

CHAPTER 5

VISITOR FROM THE SOUTH

One summer evening Typos called me. I had been freezing runner and broad beans all day and peeling, podding and blanching these things filled my days. The kitchen was full of steam and the blanching, bagging and putting the produce in the freezers filled my afternoon. The day was cooling down as the sun set, but it was still warm and I worked away in shirt sleeves.

The dogs were piled up in the yard, dozing but with the usual eye open, missing nothing. The younger puppy, India, had given up wrestling with the bigger dog's tail and was sound asleep, upside down in the dust, her body twisting with dreams.

I had stopped for a mug of tea, and once I had made it I took it to the garden with a slab of my favourite Battenberg cake. Sitting on the swing seat, I watched the swallows screaming and whizzing about overhead, and an old wolfhound, Milly's granddaughter, wandered sleepily around to me, sharing the cake, then put her head on my lap.

Into this harmony Typos' call arrived, almost splitting my head with its urgency and strength. It was lucky that my tea mug was nearly empty because I dropped it onto the grass below me, bending forward as I fought back that sick feeling. It passed when I received the thought in my head ' now' and 'eat', which I found intriguing. Never before had she told me what to do, apart from meet her.

I wandered into the kitchen and cut myself a lump of bread and cheese, shoving it into my pocket. I was not really hungry then anyway, having just had cake. With the doors locked and the dogs settled and briefed, I gave the horses in the paddock below a cursory look, and seeing that all was well, I started up the hill.

The road that day was dusty, the dandelions on the road edge had dusted leaves and the wild garlic and clumps of cow parsley were almost drooping. A few village children cycled about noisily joshing each other, enjoying the remaining heat and setting sun.

The lane to our top fields is rather steep, and my progress, you could say, was slow. Reaching the top gate, I stopped for a moment to get my breath and looked back down on the village and across the hill. To the south, a faint thin ribbon of sea was just visible in the half light, and back behind me the hills above the nearest village looked stripped where the silage grass had been cut.

A few clouds gently wandered inland, being pushed by a light wind which was playing with what hair I have left. In front of me the field of ewes with their now well-grown lambs running about lifted their heads to look at me. Realising that today I was no threat to their dignity, they put their heads back down to pull at the grass, bleating in deep voices with mouths full.

I climbed the gate, not bothering with the padlock, then walked across to the barn, kicking at a dock leaves as I went. I will admit that even at my age, if I find a dandelion clock hiding in the grass, I pick it and blow on it to see the time. Pathetic, I know.

As I have told you before, Typos and I were surprised here before by a woman from the village and today, as always now, I looked around to check that I was alone.

In the barn, kneeling down, I began the call. I remember being amazed how quickly she appeared. I had hardly begun and she was there, and of all things, and you will not believe this, she was almost laughing. How, you may be thinking? I can hear your disbelief. But having been years with her, I can tell you that she was excited.

With her arrival, I was straight away struggling to my feet.

'What is up with you then?' she thought to me. I threw my arms out wide and then went over to give her scaly neck its usual squeeze. She was obviously excited, her back legs, despite her size, dancing up and down. I watched them carefully, keeping out of the way of the razor talons which chewed at the turf.

'We go, further than usual, but still a way. A chance' she blurted out, much more visibly excited than normal.

'Hang on, slow down, what? And what is happening?'

I stood back from her, looking at her sides moving in and out with excited breathing. Small flames flickered from her breath.

'We meet the other rider, he and his Wakaramasta are near. We go to meet.'

'What, there is another like me?' I was stunned.

'We go on. It is still a way.... will take long time. Have you fed? I have.'

She rolled her head to one side as she looked down at me. I was momentarily held by the lump of gristly meat caught in her front talon.

'Yes I am fine, I have got a pocket full, but...'

'On come on! It is, do you say, good, come!' she blurted out, pushing her head and neck forward and down, her wings almost at ground level. I went around, swung a leg over and wriggled down into my usual seat between the spines on her neck.

'I am fine,' I thought to her.

'We go,' she said and twitched out, giving me the usual transient burst of nausea, her wings working so hard that I could feel each muscle group working below me. We climbed up into the sky, not circling but climbing in a straight line, straight for the sea.

As we climbed it got colder, but the view held me entranced. The sun was almost kissing the sea, the red light almost painful to look at. Far below, the Channel came into view and soon Typos was over it, with a few cross-Channel ferries almost meeting in the middle. I was intrigued to see just how many vessels were slugging along, their wakes spread out behind. The sea looked remarkably calm from our height, with just the odd white-capped roller.

I wriggled my hands under my thighs as my hands got colder and gave her neck a squeeze with my legs locked around her neck.

'You well?' she thought to me, stopping her wings and gliding into the wind.

'I am fine, no problems, Where do we go?'

'The next island has taller mountains lower down. We meet them on those.'

'France? The Alps!' I exclaimed, unable to believe it.

'I do not know what you say, it is many wing beats since you have eaten' she thought again.

'Yes, do not worry, I am fine.' In fact I was already beginning to feel a tad hungry and actually cold.

'Good, we move now.' With that she half closed her wings, almost falling forward and accelerating so that the skin on my face shook with the wind force. The wind seemed to tear at my body through my clothes, watering my eyes so much that I could not really look forward. She opened her great wings nearer the ground and still going in a straight line, it seemed she eventually regained our previous height, only to dive forward at high speed again. This she repeated time and time again, with me losing count. When we were over what I realised later must have been an airport, she went higher, so much so that initially I began gasping for air and got incredibly cold. I was very glad of the heat from her obviously hot and sweaty body as I struggled to get closer to her.

She flew on until I saw ahead a mountain range which I assumed must be the Alps, topped with patches of snow. Tiny fields had been formed and from the valley bottoms they reached up the sides until with height they fizzled out and stopped.

At the same time, I became aware that another dragon was thinking to Typos. I was not able to understand any of it, so I just kept still, quiet not interfering.

'We meet soon, they are here' she thought to me. 'He is the only other, from the other part of this world, the other half… same as you for his half, with Wakaramasta, the same as me.'

'What, are you having me on?' I replied. But then there appeared in front of us a vision that had me speechless. It was initially a considerable distance away, and was lost from sight now and then as the mountains behind stopped the contrasting view; but I could soon see clearly that it was another flying dragon with a lump on its neck. It rapidly got nearer, thanks to a much faster wing rate, and was covering lots of ground. It was all black, with no colour at all. Very quickly it was just in front of us, when it began to glide, keeping the same distance from Typos. She was cruising now, her wings lazily working.

And then I realised that the lump on its neck was in fact a human form, a man, sitting there, just like me. I rubbed at my watering eyes, scarcely able to believe them.

He appeared to be wearing a squashed black hat, rather like that of a pirate, and a long black gown. I could see that it was open at the front over a slatted black waistcoat, buttoned to the neck. His legs were encased in long, black baggy trousers that flapped in the wind. Like me, his feet were buried in his dragon's neck scales, but I briefly saw as they turned and got nearer that he was wearing black sandals.

There was just enough light at our height for me to see him grinning at me from under his hat, a toothy smile. He was thin, with a sharp face, very tanned and with a thin goatee beard and thin moustache. I felt like calling out, but Typos filled my thoughts.

'You cannot talk, he is different, his tongue is wrong for you.'

I did not know what to say anyway, being somewhat tongue–tied.

'Once each Myrrdin are to meet. One from high, one from low, this is now' she thought to me. 'He is also like you Myrrdin, with his, how do you say 'dragon'?'

I looked across to see the rider from the other hemisphere lift a hand in greeting, which I echoed, lifting a hand and then hopelessly shouting out across to him 'hello'.

Now I will butt in to say, because I can imagine you smiling at this, what else could I say? I sat there frankly feeling a little awkward, as there followed many dragon thought noises, which now and then entered my mind. Looking across at him sitting so still and perfectly straight backed, he looked in perfect harmony with his mount, the wind tearing at his billowing clothes.

He looked across at me and gave me a smile, which I was happy to return. Then he put both hands together and acted out shaking them both. I was happy to copy this back, and heard across the gap a deep, rippling laugh.

'He wishes you well, good fortune, and peace' thought Typos to me.

'You must say the same back, please Typos, I wish we could speak more on the ground. Tell them to be very safe and good luck always.'

'We talk to each other and she to him, but is complete. We turn now, your one time is done.' With that, and giving each other a cursory nod, both dragons turned. I twisted around on Typos' neck just to watch the amazing speed at which they left. Soon they were just dots in the sky. Our speed seemed stationary by comparison.

Typos was now slogging back against a head wind that made her work hard, and about half way back it began to rain. This forced her to go above the cloud layer.

My hands, despite her heat, became very cold, so I had to blow on them to hold my bread roll and cheese safely. To be honest they came out of my pocket squeezed together with a lot of crushed dog biscuit crumbs, which I had forgotten. I am playing for sympathy when I say that I was freezing cold, cramped, streaming-eyed, hungry and chewing up a roll studded with dog biscuit crumbs.

Yet more important than this was the thought that I was not alone; there was another like me on this planet. It will perhaps seem odd to you, but I felt reassured. I began to sing aloud in happiness, which prompted Typos to ask if all was well.

'Yes very well, very well' I thought back, giving her neck a playful crushing squeeze with my legs. 'Very well!'

She slogged on against the rain and wind, while below us in the pitch black the odd clump of lights showed the cities up that we went over. Soon to my relief the jet black scar of the Channel was below, and it seemed we were quickly looking down at the shore lights of the English coast.

An obviously tired Typos twitched back in front of the barn, and with a lot of effort I rolled off her onto the soaking ground. My legs had seized up, and the cold seemed to have reached every part of my body. It took me a lot of effort, but with a lot of crawling and inward cursing, I used the barn side to get myself upright.

Turning around to Typos, we had what I will describe as a complete mental joining. Words are inadequate to describe it, and I will not even try. This joining is truly calming, wonderful, complete and extraordinary.

The night was over. We stood side by side as a weak sun began rising, turning the sky increasingly red from pink, and then appearing as half a disc.

With the sounds of the ewes calling their lambs and the morning chorus from the hedgerow birds beginning, I felt complete.

'That was unexpected and wonderful' I thought to her, placing a hand on her neck.

'You are soon finished. I can do a service, as you know, when you are complete' she calmly thought back.

I paused, thinking of all I had seen, and of William who would follow. I remembered Jules, who had introduced this bizarre life to me, and importantly I had been told and shown by Typos many lovely times of harmony with Freyja.

'I have to get you together with the next Myrrdin again' I thought back. 'He has to meet the watchers, see the river forces and honour them.'

I paused, wondering if it was prudent to mention her annual duty to the Wind Furies. She beat me to this.

'The Wind Furies will call soon' she thought. With this a small jet of flame flickered from her jaws. 'They are soon, you will have your Myrrdin replacement to witness.'

'Yes of course. Just call'

I did not feel able to say more, as obviously the memory of them killing her mother was too real. Even though the death had been avenged, with her friends' help, it was painful for her.

After another pause watching the rising sun with my hand on her neck, I continued. 'What do you mean, service? Is that when I die? I know that I cannot, do not, go beyond eighty five.'

'You will get another life as, how do you say, your reward. You need have no fear. If you wish I will take you back, you will see Jules, if you wish, or Freyja. I can arrange anything you think.'

Now to be honest I had worked a lot of things out, and my thoughts were, shall I say, strange, to use an understatement. Like a simpleton, I suppose, I thought to her.

'Can I take a dog, my dog, to this other life?' I held my breath. 'Or my horse friend?'

It will perhaps seem strange to you, but she bent her great neck down so that her head was on my level, and grinned.

'No, not them' she said with immense kindness. 'Their needs are different. Your successor will tell them, be there for them.'

'He is not like me, he cannot think to them,' I replied.

'Not yet, I have not finished. He will have the same gift to help him as you. I sort him.'

This was two years ago, I have shown William many extraordinary things, a few of which I will tell you about in a moment, but at that point the continuity of the Myrrdin position became evident to me. Was it strange to know the time when I would be no more? Then to be reformed, remembering nothing; seeing Jules again without remembering him, or starting a life with Freyja, and so on? You bet it was, it was weird.

Before the sun rose any further, Typos and I said our farewells until next time. I walked down off the hill, surprising the village milkman, who gave me a wave, and thinking to the dogs not to bark or serenade my arrival back. But they went berserk to see me back. There was much tail-wagging and leaping in the air with all feet airborne.

Having fed them, seen the horses and wandered around in a bit of a daze, I hit the sack. Sleep came easily, despite having my two Labradors on the bed, both dreaming, yet keeping guard.

CHAPTER 6

HORROR ON THE BATTLEFIELD

The best plans can so easily get messed up, and those I had planned for William to meet with Typos again certainly were.

On a bitingly cold autumn morning, with a really heavy frost on the ground, Will had come over to help with sawing up a load of logs for my winter fires. During the week before I had used the tractor to drag back to the lower yard some fallen limbs of a big beech, and several stumps of trees I had dropped the year before. On hearing his scooter arrive and seeing the dogs stir themselves from beds in front of the Aga, I knew he had arrived. Lifting the old kettle from the hotplate on the cooker's edge and placing it on the Aga's boiling plate, I reached down two mugs from the wall cupboard and fished out two tea-bags.

The compulsory brew was ready as he came into the kitchen, bending down to greet the ecstatically tail-wagging dogs.

'How you doing, Will? Had a good week? Here, have a brew' I said, smiling and passing a mug along the worktop.

'Yes, thanks, boy it is cold out there! Not a bad week I suppose, usual stuff, boring lectures. I'll be glad when I finish, it is getting a bit intense now for my exams next summer. Got to finish my college selection. It's a bit tricky to be honest. Still not sure what I will do.'

'Just choose as if nothing was happening' I said, looking up at him. 'You being my replacement will easily fit. The job fitted with me and Jules before me, and I am certain everyone before him. You'll be surprised. Carry on just as you were before you knew.'

I paused, sipping the red hot tea, then shoved the biscuit tin over to him.

'I took over from a man called Jules, a really nice useful chap, who taught me such a lot. He was a farm worker, doing hedging, planting, tractor stuff, and well, I inherited this smallholding from him. I've muddled along being a bit self-sufficient, doing the odd job, you could say. Typos calls now and then, not very often, and the other duties seem to fit during the year. What I am trying to say is that I am sure college and then a job will fit fine. All right?

Will smiled back. 'I'm more happy with this now I've thought about it' he said, grabbing another biscuit. He looked down at the dogs, who sat looking adoringly up, tails wagging, begging as always.

'I'm going to have you meet with Typos again soon' I said. 'And you and I have to travel to a meeting with some other watchers soon, people like us.'

He rummaged around in the tin until he found a chocolate one and looked up.

'What, are there many? A whole group?' He looked intrigued.

'No, just one for each country in the British Isles' I smiled back. Then, putting a more serious face on, 'also, just you and I will eventually meet the water forces, shall I say. And you have to witness Typos negotiating with the Wind Furies.'

At this point I left it at that, having no wish to explain all about Typos' mother's dealings with them and the revenge she had enacted on them.

'Come on, let's get going, push it in' I said. I finished my tea and put the cup in the sink, then went across to wrestle my boots on. The dogs all woke up, or at least pretended to, and with a turn of the key in the back door we walked down to the yard.

The grass was white and crisp, with the odd sheet of thin crackling ice where odd patches of standing water had frozen overnight. All was still, with not even a breeze moving the remaining leaves, which were hanging frozen. Further below us in the orchard, a great twisting mess of starlings flew to and fro, seeming to argue about something.

With me carrying the chainsaw, and Will the tin of fuel and joshing with the dogs, we walked into the yard to start. We had worked together before, both wearing gloves and ear defenders. After the usual cursing, pulling and fiddling with the choke, then more cursing, at last the saw smoked into life.

The dogs amused themselves as Will fed the workhorse with new branches, and we worked our way through. The big root bowls on the ground needed to be half cut, rolled over and cut again. Our communication, with heads covered, ears blocked and the saw growling, was limited to hand signals and gesturing.

We had been going for I suppose a couple of hours when out of the corner of my eye I saw Will bend, turn and half fall, throwing up as he went over. I snapped the saw off. I knew that Typos was calling. As I have said before, the call fills your head and many times it has made me throw up as well. Luckily not this time; I just heard an insistent 'now now'.

Pulling gloves off and ear pieces out I went over to Will and put an arm around his shoulder. Typos was thinking 'now' then again 'now', with obvious urgency.

'You all right Will?' I asked him. 'It always does that to me. She wants us, come on!'

He straightened up, wiping his mouth with the back of his hand. 'Is it always like that? Do you ever get used to it? What is it all about?' He spat out a load of phlegm and looked across at me.

'No, it is only the first few times' I lied, glad that the watching dogs could not correct me. We bundled all the kit together, locked it in the feed room, settled the dogs in their beds and set off up the hill to the barn. I set a brisk pace as I could manage, although to be honest, with even my best efforts Will was just idling along.

Catching my breath now and then and momentarily pausing, I turned to him.

'Now are you all right with this? She called you as well, and when it's your turn, that is when I am not here, that's what she will do. It is not to say you have to drop everything, in fact you will have a set place, a private place to call her, but sometimes, like now, she can be insistent.'

Between breaths I carried on, Will walking beside me, keeping quiet, just nodding. 'I will teach you how to call her if you have need later, but, and this is really important, you must never call her unless the need is great. She will call when she needs your official witness, that's your job. You will do this for all humans as representative. Obviously today she has need.'

I stopped by the lane edge, just short of the field gate.

'I cannot say what we will see. You have got to be more than a bit grown up about this.' I looked him straight in the eye and he looked back, perhaps more than a little worried.

'It can be strange perhaps. It can be dreadful, but you are there to witness and boy oh boy, having a dragon looking after you as your best mate is quite a perk! Come on over to the barn and you can watch and listen to me call her.'

We walked across the top of the hill to the barn, sending two pheasants out of the field edge. 'Always out of season, and no gun when they do that' laughed Will, swinging an imaginary shotgun after them.

'I would have missed anyway' I smiled back. 'I'm a hopeless shot now. Never mind, it's nice to see them'.

I inwardly smiled at how relaxed he now seemed, given that he was about to see Typos again. How the young adapt!

We walked up to my old barn, which is three-bayed and open-fronted. In front were patches of frozen mud where the animals had poached up the ground. Amongst the dock stalks standing in the frosted grass, the odd frozen thistle stood, and on the furthest side a big frozen puddle lay across the way in.

'Look, I'm so stiff and worn out now that I have to use the barn upright to lower myself down, and call her kneeling' I said. 'It's not a bad idea to do this anyway as sometimes the force of her arrival can be immense. It can knock you over. Kneel by me here.'

I pointed alongside me as I lowered myself. He now looked a bit more serious again.

'Come on.' I pointed. 'Let's call her, it will be fine. 'I'll teach you this chant later as I said, but in two halves so that you won't call her by accident. Finally, do not be a muppet. She needs room - do not call her indoors!'

I smiled at him, making sure that the message had gone home, and waving a finger to force it in.

'Make sure you're on your own, too. I got caught out once and Typos had to deal with it. I'm not going to tell you how now, but it could have been a bit embarrassing to say the least.'

He had relaxed a bit and gave me a half laugh.

'Right, this chant, or whatever you want to call it, her call, can be said out loud, or thought in your head. It doesn't matter, the join with her is there. Repeat and repeat it, until it seems to take over. I do, and I've always kept my eyes shut. You will feel, then hear, her arrival. Finally face that way, I really do not know why, it seems a bit unnecessary, but do - I was told to.' I pointed to the north-west. 'I suppose towards Wales. Anyway, I start.'

Will knelt beside me with me grabbing his hand, and with both our eyes tight shut, I started the call, out loud so he could hear. This repetition I have now carried out many times over the years and still I feel the excitement begin to rise, as soon, almost on cue the chant gathers its own momentum, filling the air with its pagan repetitions and rhyme, and getting a power of its own. I felt my lungs would burst, as with my vocal chords almost appealing for mercy, the pressure grew and grew. Through it all, I felt Will begin to waver and shake beside me. Then all grew quiet, the birds stopped singing and all the sheep and cows were hushed.

Without the need to open my eyes I could feel her there, hear her talons rip the grass, and smell that distinctive lemony-leathery smell. Giving Will's hand a squeeze, I said, 'Open your eyes, we are complete, she is here.'

I opened my eyes to catch Typos looking at us, and then quickly look at Will. He was looking with saucer eyes, mouth jammed open, and noticeably beginning to dribble. He remained kneeling alongside, and started to shake. He looked at me wide eyed, then wiped with his free hand at his chin.

'You are here as asked, we go, now on' commanded Typos. She half smiled and a small burst of flames issued from between her teeth. Even though her head was turned down at the time, the heat could still be felt, and a wisp of hay in front of her caught alight, smoking a thin trail into the air.

'Come on Will, we are going with her today, it seems.' I twisted and wriggled to my feet. Walking over to her, I put my arms around her neck, and looked back at Will. He had got up and moved behind a barn stanchion, peeping out at us.

'Come on' I beckoned, giving him a big smile. He moved a little. 'What do you mean, going with her?' he whispered, beginning to tremble, his legs shaking.

'It's all right, come on, it's our job. She is really comfy, in the right place.'

'What - on her?' said Will in horror.

'Yes, come on!' I beckoned, and I do not mind admitting that perhaps I was a little short, my tone perhaps not so soft. He walked over, and I was aware that at that point Typos took control. Looking at the ground, not up at her, Will came over to me, and I gave him a leg up onto her lowered neck.

'It is really important that you do not get off, or fall off, until she finishes' I said. I gave his foot a squeeze. 'Now move down the bus.' I was wondering how on earth I would get behind him. How had Jules done it?

After a lot of clutching and wriggling, I managed to get snug behind, between her large neck spines, where I felt very at home. I put my arms around Will, grabbing him safe.

'Now, wrap your legs under her neck... by the way I forgot to ask, are you horsy? Have you ridden?'

'No not at all' he whispered. 'Is this safe? I feel like I could fall off!'

I laughed. 'Do not bother to do that, you are mind linked to her, no need to whisper.'

'That is right, we go' thought Typos, and with a massive bound from her powerful back legs we were airborne. She immediately turned, and I pulled Will's body over to match her angle. He tensed.

'It's just like leaning on a bike, you will get there. I have never, ever been able to anticipate it, but she is so big, you will get there, don't worry.'

Typos flew on, the big muscles in her back and neck flexing under our hands. Each downbeat of her wings could be felt right through your backbone. I felt Will relax a little, beginning to be entranced by the power and the view.

She had climbed up into a wispy cloud layer, but amusingly, on the way up to it, Will almost waved and called out to a couple on the ground. At the very moment I was about to explain, Typos thought, 'This is not your now, we are a moment behind, they will not see.'

'See what?' Will turned to me.

'I will explain when we get back. Dragons twitch, they can jiggle time, I told you - remember?'

He turned back without comment and I realised how much I now took for granted, and how much I still had to explain.

Soon the channel came into view with the usual boats plying to and fro. Further out two massive container ships left ruler-straight wakes.

'Where do you need to be?' asked Will.

'I am called to help, we go back further.'

I started to explain at the same moment as Typos twitched savagely back, making me feel sick, as usual, but poor Will chucked up heavily. Luckily he had the presence of mind to shove his head over her side. I grabbed the back of his jacket, pulling him more upright.

'That's fine, my lad' I said in reassurance. 'You all right? Sometimes it does that to me too.'

He wiped the back of his face with his hand. 'I really did not like that' he whispered back to me in the strengthening wind. I could see him looking at the sea below, with an element of fear on his face.

'You are fine?' thought Typos, 'You have a problem?'

'No, I feel we are fine. Where are we?'

'This is what you call the start, the beginning of your century. The time when you all tried to kill.'

'What, the war?' I exclaimed.

'Yes, the humans' first major time of madness here, not the second, or ones before' she thought back to us. I shook Will through his jacket and leaned forward, nearly shouting in his ear.

'Look this is important, we are back in time, you must not, really not, fall or get off her. You must understand. I was nearly stranded in the past by her mother when I fell. Now don't worry, but you simply must not. Do you really understand this? Will, it is so important.'

He nodded back, his face deathly white. Frankly I felt petrified myself.

The cloud grew in thickness, almost to the point where you felt you could have got off Typos and walked on it. Looking down through the gaps revealed a dirty brown landscape with a long muddy scar stretching for miles below us. Looking carefully when gaps allowed, you could just make out the odd vehicle moving along a twisting road, then a ragged column of people, then further on a marching group of what I took to be soldiers.

Typos then began to fly higher, her wings pumping hard. The temperature dropped and Will tried to turn to me. He waved with his hands at his chest, then his mouth, making it plain that he was finding breathing hard.

'It will be for a reason, it will not be long, it will pass, go with it' I tried to reassure him. I gave his back an encouraging rub, but inwardly I was wondering.

Then from below us we heard the loud crumping of ordnance and the hiss of passing shells. Looking down, innumerable small fires could be seen. There was mud everywhere. Even at this height, the whole scene below us looked truly ghastly.

I had seen enough on TV and read enough to know that we were watching the horrors of trench warfare. Will obviously realised this too. He was trying to turn to me. His right hand sought mine, his face truly petrified.

I do not mind admitting that for me to have involved this young man and make him witness such horror made me question myself and this whole position. Yet through it all came the thought that below us men, or more likely boys, of his own age were dying in horrible ways, even as we watched. I could not say anything to him; I was at a loss. I put my hands on his shoulders as he looked down.

The reason for Typos' climb became evident as below us we heard the hissing flight of shells. The air up here was thin, and my breathing was laboured. The warmth from Typos' muscles was welcome, and I pushed one hand beneath my leg against her neck.

'We go down soon. My call is soon, my friends are too busy with this madness' she thought to me. She had felt me moving, and at this moment she locked her wings out straight and began a long, slow glide down. The back edge of the cloud got thinner, eventually finishing and giving us a better view of the countryside below. The fields here were green and unmarked.

I twisted round to look back under the cloud edge at the horror we had left behind. At this point I do not mind admitting to you that I cried out in fear, remembering the horrible demons, ghouls, call them what you will, that Shola had fought at the plague pits above my home village in Dorset. For along the edge of the muddy scar, truly hideous forms swung staves and what looked like large axes as they went up and down the line. Gangly creatures with large grotesque heads and yellow eyes were slobbering and drooling.

'They fight for souls' thought Typos to me.

I watched in amazement as another dragon appeared above them. It was jet black, smaller than Typos, with a fast wing rate, and it was bellowing a great plume of fire.

'I turn, you watch for a moment' she said. She arced through the air and Will and I watched in horror as she dived at the ground, rolling on her side to lash with her front talons at one of the creatures. It clutched at its middle and flung its head back, and fell dying in screaming defiance. The dragon flipped over and shot back up to turn on another.

'Enough, this is horrible, I cannot do this!' screamed Will, clutching back at me.

'You can. We will win' thought Typos back, with a power I had never felt in her before. 'Why your people do this is alien to us. We fight for your, how do you say next life? You are here to witness, enough.'

This was her final thought, almost as a command, stating the obvious. To be honest to you, for me, having seen so much with her and her mother, it was not new, but that did not diminish the vile sights.

'I will explain later, do not worry' I said to Will. 'I did say that sometimes it is horrible. Typos has been called to help, we are to witness, that is all.' I paused. 'Look, if there is a force for good then there must be a force for evil, you will see everything now.'

Will turned away from me, but not before I had seen his great fear. Tears starting to course down from his red eyes. He lifted his right hand and waved it aimlessly in the air at me. He seemed to shrink into Typos' neck, his shoulders shaking as he began to sob. I felt helpless, just wishing he had not had to see such a harrowing spectacle.

At this point we had glided down to a few hundred feet, and appeared to be over a small airfield.

'It is near here we are called for' came Typos' thought. A perimeter road of sorts passed below us, and a small village passed underneath with a group of people running along a road, obviously with great purpose. I felt Will suddenly stiffen, straining to see forward, not saying anything but starting to point, almost wave.

'I see it' I reassured him.

Beyond us a fire burned on the ground and around it there patrolled another gangrenous creature. It loped around the fire, trying now and then to dart in. Green in colour, with limbs looking ridiculously long, it was throwing its head back to howl at nothing in particular. It was revolting.

However, it now saw us. It straightened up, waving its staff in a defiant gesture and howling abuse. As we got nearer it was obvious to me that we were above a burning airship, its gondola just visible on the edge of the burning steel framework that had carried the balloon. A gas dirigible had ignited and crashed down; through the smoke and roaring flames I could just make out twisted bodies.

'Just concentrate on Typos' I shouted to Will. 'Stay with her movements, keep light, don't interfere.'

He nodded, and at that moment that she put on an amazing turn of speed which brought instant watery eyes, obstructing our vision. I grabbed Will tightly round his middle and clenched my legs into Typos' neck as we fell, rushing towards the ground and the ghastly creature. It hurled a stream of abuse at us, then, bringing its arm back, it flung the staff towards us. It passed with a strange hum harmlessly below.

At the point when I was convinced she had overcooked it and we would crash into the ground, Typos rolled sideway and all four legs shot out from under her with talons bared. The noise as they ripped into the vile creature I will never forget. At the same time I was amazed to hear Will yell – whether in triumph or encouragement it was hard to tell. On thinking back, the rightness of her actions and her need had become apparent to him; he was starting to see the hidden importance of them for the human race.

I gripped us both like mad as in a length she turned and racked the now writhing creature with a fiery blast, so hot that we were both forced to protect our eyes with both hands momentarily letting go. Then, using her speed, she shot up into the air and turned to look down.

The few people running along the road had arrived, and they struggled to fight the heat as they stood looking in frustration at the burning mess.

'That is my call done' thought Typos to us. 'My friends you have seen are busy, but it is not my call. We are done. Return.'

'Is that it? Do we go back? What about behind us?' The questions poured out from Will, who was obviously now beginning to be a little excited, shall I say, by what he had seen.

'Yes, we finish' thought Typos, and without any notice she twitched back.

The weather was instantly warmer. A balmy late afternoon sun shone through a thin cloud cover, but as we flew on, the cold icy weather we had left behind started chilling our bones.

Will had been excitedly chattering about what he had seen, but as we crossed the Channel, he became silent. Looking back it is plain to me that the reality, the shock of all he had seen, was starting to affect him.

As the field came into sight, Typos thought to me, 'The new Myrrdin will stay, I have need.'

'Fine' I thought back, wondering what was going to happen, but trusting her fully. She landed with the usual shower of mud and ripped grass.

'It will be fine, stay with her Will,' I said as with a lot of wriggling I landed on the frosted grass. 'Go with her, just for a while, she wants to show you things, explain things, I am sure. I will be here waiting. Typos will look after you - treasure you. Isn't that right?'

I looked at her and as I have said before she smiled back, and then she twitched out, gone. I am happy, or shall I say brave enough, to tell you that this moment was the second terribly sad moment I have felt. I was glad that Will and Typos were together; after all, my time is nearly done. It did bring home to me how privileged I had been, how different life had been.

This account must not get maudlin, as I have written before, but to be honest, as I sit here with dog at my feet recalling all that has happened, it is difficult to avoid it.

I wandered rather aimlessly about, walking over to check sheep and kicking patches of frozen nettles, for what seemed ages, but was in fact possibly only twenty minutes.

'We come' came the call from Typos. I walked back to the barn in time to see my dragon friend carrying a bemused but soon smiling Will.

'You all right, big boy?' I called out as he slithered off her neck, and I was so pleased to see him turn and stand hugging her scaly neck.

'He is complete. Now all gifts are present, he knows more now. I will need you for the wind forces soon. I will call.' She turned to look at me. 'I go, be safe.'

With that she twitched out, leaving an obviously tired Will slumping down on the frozen grass.

'When are we? I have been two days with her' he muttered.

'Strange as it may seem, and to add to your purgatory, it was only about a quarter of an hour.' I laughed as I pulled him to his feet, and he looked at me bemused.

'Yes I am being straight, honest, you see what she can do? Come on, we need a big load of toast and a mug, no mugs, of tea. Actually I make some rather special bickies, the recipe was given to me by Jules. They have, let's say, a special edge to them. It's time you tackled them.'

He looked at me with just the hint of a smile. 'This is weirder than I could ever imagine. You have been like this all your life?'

'Yep, and you wait until we get in and you natter to the dogs, it will blow your mind!' I laughed out loud and gave him a shove as we set off home.

Now in other accounts I have added a bit for any doubting Thomases who may read this account. Go to your history books. Look at September 1915 or thereabouts, in France, and you will find an account of an airship caught in a violent stormy updraft. The released hydrogen to counter this was probably ignited by lightning or static. Sadly all nineteen crew were killed. That is what Typos was called to deal with, and Will witnessed.

CHAPTER 7

A PERSONAL CONFESSION

If you have found and read my previous memories, you will know that every year in March or thereabouts my job is to witness for you the water forces, or some of them. I have to admit that following an accident with Shola, I fouled up badly. In the interlude when I was not attending, some three years, the climate of the West Country was way too dry, with crops and livestock suffering.

It became painfully obvious to me that these dances had had to be witnessed by a chosen person for the harmony of natural forces. Luckily, with Typos' help, and by examining an old journal I had kept, the timing and need of my visits was soon worked out.

During the last decades of these magical mornings I have been honoured to see wonderful events and the most delightful light forms. Initially the previous Merlin had introduced them to me; in fact he taught me everything, and I still miss his calm help and common sense.

He had been supported by a family he worked for, in particular by his boss's wife Jane. She confided in me soon after his death that she had been very fond of him. They had developed a genuine friendship, but worryingly he hinted that she vaguely knew that each year he had to deal with what she called 'water fairies'.

When she put her knowledge to me, I was at a loss how to deal with it. I answered flippantly, only too aware that she could see through my joking answers.

A tall, willowy, bubbly blonde with a twinkling eye, Jane was fifteen years older than me. She wore a distinctive perfume which hung in the air around her, and I do not mind admitting that she as she aged she seemed to get prettier each year. She had three small children when I first met. As is so often the way these days, sadly, she and her husband amicably separated, but remained still very good friends. She was clever and didn't miss a trick.

I gathered from her questions that she had worked out that Jules had something major going on in his life. Then I arrived on the scene and for a couple of years I was always with him, which seemed just as mysterious.

Once I met her walking back from a local village where she had been lunching with friends. I couldn't avoid her; it would have been blatantly rude if I had not spoken to her, so we walked home together. As we walked she told me much of her friendship with Jules and started quizzing me about his 'other work' .

Of course, I told her as little as I could. As she turned to go, she drew me to her and kissed me full on the lips. Then she stood back, her hands either side of my face, and looked me straight in the eye.

'Carry on his work for me, for all of us,' she said. With that she turned and walked off, her big straw hat trailing ribbons and leaving her intoxicating perfume hanging in the air.

I stood watching her go, and after about fifty yards she turned and blew a kiss to me, then carried on homeward. After that we became quite close, thanks to our link with Jules.

* * *

Thinking back now, it was perhaps five years after Jules died that my annual visit for the water forces was changed in my memory for good. I had got into the habit of taking a dog with me on these mornings. They were used to trailing behind at a discreet distance, amusing themselves until the return walk, when they gambolled by me, chatting away.

We had to leave the house very early, before the sun rose. After waking myself up with a big mug of tea and sharing nearly a whole packet of biscuits with Bumble, my German Pointer and doggie mate, we left the terriers in their beds by the Aga, locked the door and walked down through the orchard. The grass was sopping wet and I was glad I had my waders were on, although walking with them can be awkward and at times noisy.

Bumble ran ahead, leading me down to the field gate, where he waited. He turned his head as I arrived and I thought to him, 'I'll go ahead as normal, you just follow and keep in touch. It will happen somewhere along here. Last year we were nearly on the beach. Remember?'

In the laid-back way he had, he sent back, 'Fine, trot on, I'll be here or somewhere near'. His languid attitude always made me smile, and I almost laughed out loud. Reaching down, I gave him the usual hug; then, with his stumpy tail wagging, he wandered back upriver, now and then turning to see if I had started.

The riverbank vegetation had not really got growing yet, but progress along the bank was blocked in places by field fences entering the river to stop stock going around. My long waders allowed me to splash along the water's edge in places as I watched the flow ahead, trying to avoid deeper pools.

The water is always gin clear, flowing fast in places and making the weed wave in the current. The river gets wider and slower as it leaves my home fields, losing some of its chatter. It crosses through rich grass fields, where several cows started as I appeared, their heads coming up to survey the intruder. One bellowed to the herd and turned its great head to the farmhouse, then back to me. I called a gentle reassurance and heads went back down, with long tongues ripping again at the wet grass.

The deep blue sky was now turning to pale pink. A large skein of geese went over, the lead bird rowing through the air while the following birds' wings made an occasional whistle.

As I walked, a heron noiselessly sprang up and flew upstream. As it looked nonchalantly back at me, a large shot of guano squirted out.

Each year the location varies, as I have written; sometimes it happens virtually on the beach where the sea fights with the river, but often much further upstream. That year I had just got to the start of the big flood plain and could see the lights of the coastal town in the far distance. The road lights were not yet out, and a few shops still had their all night lights on.

In the distance the few trees stood as black silhouettes, and with a bit of imagination I could imagine the far-off sea grinding on the shingle beach.

Then I saw it; a hundred yards away, close by the river's edge. A blue flame began dancing on the water, nearly touching the reeds. I knew that it had begun. I thought back to Bumble to tell him to stop and wait where he was. Then I settled to watch on the bank edge, sitting quietly down on my waxproof.

It was perfectly quiet, except for the sounds of the river. The water was making a faint gurgling around a caught-up tree stump. In the distance I could hear a milkman's float, and further downstream a group of mallards could be heard waking up and beginning to argue about life.

The flame began to grow in intensity, and was soon joined by three more. They left the water and grew to a couple of feet high. They gave off no heat and made just a faint hiss. These were the 'fairies', to use a term Mrs Andrews had referred to, that Jules had shown me, and I have witnessed them now every year for decades.

They have also carried a much more relevant meaning for me, which I will eventually explain.

As always, at this point the flames began almost to dance, relating to each other, slowly circling, remaining the same colour. They moved upstream to where we sat. They grew in height, still giving off no heat, and the riverbank vegetation did not seem affected at all.

Some years ago, when I missed these events for a while owing to my injury and spell in hospital, I returned to a rather special display. The flames moved off seawards and returned with a much larger column of flame, towering and spiralling, which almost danced right up to me. I was, and still am, awed by this sight. I was honoured to be chosen to see it each year, whilst most of the country was asleep or just waking.

The flames almost bowed to me and slowly diminished until they soundlessly disappeared, and with that the river come back to life.

That morning as I pulled myself up, two blackbirds barged past, 'pinking' at each other, and downstream mallards began to argue again. I can remember stretching each arm up, as through the morning hazy light Bumble trotted.

'I saw it in the distance, strange, very strange and no smell' came his thoughts. He moved to the river's edge, his nose twitching, and I could hear the air as he sucked it in over his tongue.

'No, it is awesome isn't it, always the same, each year.' I paused, giving his coat a brush with my hand, lost in thought and remembering.

'Come on boss' he said, giving his neck a vigorous jockey rub. 'You hungry? Race you back for a fry.'

He smiled and gambolled off, turning to look back before being distracted by a pile of logs that needed an urgent smelling. I walked on, lost in thought, watching the sun coming up, missing cowpats and then going back to the river edge to get past some fence rails.

The light was full now. I stopped momentarily to watch a pair of woodpigeons squabble in a hawthorn bush, and then saw a thin, mangy fox turn and look at me before running on.

Bumble brought me sharply back to reality as up ahead I heard him bark once, and then the low growl started that he used to mean business. I walked quickly up, bending underneath the beech branches that grew down and over this stretch. Soon I could see him, rigid ahead of me, hackles up, just casting an eye back as he heard me behind.

'What is it, what's up mate?' I thought.

'Up ahead, person hiding, can hear and just smell on the wind. Waiting for you, bad... be careful!'

'What? It's early.'

'I am sure, shall I go now and fight?' His hackles came up, his legs stiff.

'No, hang on a minute until we are sure, it may be no problem.' At times a dog's defensive attitude is a treasure, and more than once I have been glad to have such a mate with me.

'Come on, we'll go together, you go first, I'll follow,' I said. He started stiffly walking ahead of me. By his posture it was obvious that he was on the point of pouncing. I followed as close as possible, but the path narrowed, passing through a mass of brambles, dead nettle stalks and the odd stunted holly bush.

'A stronger smell... of flowers' Bumble thought to me.

'Peter, is that you?' It was a voice I recognised straight away.

'Mrs Andrews – Jane! What are you doing here?'

'It's all right mate, I know her, not a problem' I let Bumble know. He went ahead, pushing through the thorny edge, his tail starting to jerk side to side, as with her arms up to protect her face, she pushed her way out. She bent down to give Bumble a pat and then looked up with a smile.

'See, I found you' she said.

That morning her hair looked, to be honest, a bit wild, roughly pulled back with an Alice band off her face. No make-up, which left her face looking a bit more open and whiter. Her blue eyes shone like small jewels. She was wearing a long coat of rough tweed, and her feet were buried in big wellingtons.

It is strange the things you remember, but now her perfume began to fill the air, floral, delicate and distinctive. I suppose on reflection, the combination of unexpected discovery, our joint friendship and that perfume enraptured me.

'What do you mean, you been watching out for me?'

'Well... for years, doing this, your river duty' she smilingly said, as she began to walk to me. Her hands left her side and she placed them on either side of my face.

'No need to say anything' she murmured and kissed me full on the lips.

* * *

I was younger then, she was pretty, we shared a few things, and I suppose I was gullible or keen, whatever you want to say. I was not unduly worried by her attention. Was I looking for excuses? Possibly.

No. it was right for us both, not hurting anyone, and her death years ago means she is safe now. Yes, that was my first horrible sorrow.

For the righteous, all names I have used are changed, her children have their own, and by the time you find this book it will be years later anyway.

'Come this way, bring your dog, I'll make you some breakfast' she said, taking my hand and pulling me gently along the path. 'Gosh, your hands are really cold, you need warming. Come on.'

I suppose, to be honest, I meekly followed on, with her leading and turning now and then to smile at me. Bumble ran ahead as we walked to her kitchen door.

'Put him in that stable with my dogs, he'll be fine. I'll put the kettle on. Come on in then, kick your waders off by the door, there's a boot jack there.'

I settled Bumble, and walked up to the door. Through the

window she saw me and beckoned me in, kettle in hand. The antique door creaked as I opened it, and I stooped so as not to bang my head on the old oak door beam.

The kitchen was warm, smelling already of rashers of bacon frying in a pan on the Aga. A black and very hairy cat was fast asleep in a basket by the stove and walking over to it, I scratched its ear.

'That's Winston, he's an ancient,' she said, smiling. She poured boiling water into the teapot, the plume of steam covering her face.

'I'll do you a couple of eggs, all right? You must be starving. Whatever time did you get up?'

'Oh, thanks, you don't have to, but that's really kind, thanks. I got up a while ago, woke early, I often take a dog along the river. It's a nice walk.'

This produced gales of laughter. She sat down, still with her coat on, with bare feet, the coat opening to her knees.

'Look Peter, I've followed you. I've known about this week for years. I tried following Jules before, and I tried to follow you as well. I have to be honest, I knew pretty well where you were this morning, but not how far down the river you go.'

She got up, broke four eggs into the frying pan and pushed the bacon aside.

'Come on, have a seat' she said, pointing at the kitchen table. 'Sunny side up all right?'

I nodded. I remember feeling very comfy, really enjoying the tea, and then devouring the bacon and eggs. Our conversation never returned at that moment to the river meeting. We were just relaxing, teasing and joking with each other. At one point I do remember her saying 'I'm getting warmer now' and undoing the top of her coat, to show her milky white skin. Later I must admit to badly stifling a yawn with the back of my hand. That did not go unnoticed.

Without any discussion, she pushed her chair back, stood up and walked around to me, putting her hand out.

'Come on, I saw that' she said, and then with a soft whisper, 'Do not say anything.' I got to my feet, pushing my chair back, and it made a grating noise on the flagstones. Then she started to remove her coat, to show me that under it she was completely naked. Her coat dropped to the floor and a young man was led upstairs.

At this point I will not tell you more, other than to say that this, perhaps, was part of her plan; to finally find out the missing elements in the facts she knew. Jules and I, and now Will, shared this duty for humankind for our patch of Great Britain.

Did she find out more? Well I have to say that she did learn a little more as time went on. She and I became very close. Yes, I am going to be discreet.

However I feel safe now, maybe I'm also more comfortable about explaining fully to you why the river flames are my future.

CHAPTER 8

THE LADY BY THE STREAM

So this is the portion of my memories I have thought long and hard about; after all, I could hardly talk it over with just anyone. I have spent days wandering about, driving my dogs and horse mad through my incommunicado life, and I will rest content only when it is recorded and written. As I have said, it will be hidden for somebody to find in the years ahead, when any danger to friends and relatives is long past.

Only a few years after discovering Jane Andrews, it began, that knowledge that completely changed my future, made me rethink my relationship with Jules and now, with only a limited time left to act as the current Myrddin, to get this account finished.

On one of those rare summer days when it was actually hot, dogs listlessly trying to sleep in the shade, horses under the trees in the home paddocks head to tailing to keep flies off, I walked down to the river's edge, clutching a blanket. It was my plan to 'catch some rays', and I carried a book, a few tins of beer, my old sunglasses and yes, a packet of the pineapple chunk sweets that Jules had got me going on.

The sky was bright blue, no clouds in sight, and the sun burned down. A few swallows flew about, thermalising and chasing the odd daddy long legs lower down. I stood watching them for a while. They always seem so joyful, screaming at each other as they showed off.

The fields are sloping here and walking can be difficult, so now and then I had to put everything down for a while, supporting myself with my hands, always finding, it seemed, prickly thistles. Following my eventful life, as you may have read, I am not the world's most mobile human being.

Along the river bank, clumps of the wretched Himalayan balsam which I had not been able to reach with the brush cutter stood, their admittedly pretty pinkish-purple flowers hanging down, besieged by bumble bees and hardly moving in the faint airs. The river here is only perhaps a foot deep, gin clear, the fronds of weed waving in the current. Further along I heard a plop as a water vole jumped in.

Further downstream the river slows into a deeper pool, and on the edge I watched a small brown trout rise and suck in a passing struggling fly; then it turned tail and shot away, back under a clump of osier roots.

In the distance could be heard the occasional lowing of cows, and up on my hill in the distance I heard the odd grumble from my sheep. Finding a reasonably flat bit by the water's edge I spread the rug out, and as I settled the church bells began their on-the-hour peal. Otherwise all was calm, and I have no problem admitting that after struggling with my book and polishing off the best part of the sweets, my eyes closed. It was one of those moments that cannot be fought with, and sleep quickly followed.

I have no idea now how long I nodded off for, but I awoke with a start as a familiar voice roused me. In my befuddled state, it seemed impossible; it was Typos.

Pulling myself up to a sitting position and rubbing sleep from my eyes, I looked about. Just when I thought I must have been dreaming, her voice came again.

'I am behind, in this what do you say... river' she said. I pulled myself around and laughed straight away. There, paddling her toes in the water, was my dragon.

'What are you here for, you lunatic, you'll be seen!' I laughed and shouted to her.

'None can see I am down' she answered. 'I have a need for you… just for you.... could not call, it is surprise I think.'

Now she had never done this to me before, for she had always called first. Now, thinking about it, she must have been watching and waiting for her moment, which had now arrived.

With a bit of inelegant wrestling I got to my feet, pulling my shirt back on, and with a final jump I managed to fling myself out into the river and grab her neck.

'What are you doing here?' I said. I pulled myself up onto her neck, helped by the bank height and her bending down. 'You normally call first, so I can prepare. Is something wrong?'

Calming thought flooded out of her, and I squeezed her neck, still giggling to myself at the absurdity of the concept and the way she was shuffling her feet, looking down at the ripples and obviously enjoying the novelty. She half-heartedly lifted her head to snap at a swallow, while the house martins were dive-bombing and heckling at her.

'I am to take you to meet someone, she has seen you... watched.'

She paused but not long enough to let me begin to talk back. 'It is on this river but back upstream, we go and find her.'

'But you will be seen, I mean does she know you, is it all right?' I wondered what this was leading to.

'It is fine, she is not - how do you say - she is not of your now. She saw you often with another woman, and has watched you for years on the river. The thing I cannot see, each year, you know that event that you have to attend, we found the time - well one of them.'

She stopped, bending her head around to look back at me. 'You have been chosen to know and meet, it is safe.'

With her being so definite, I settled down on her neck and she gently twitched out, for once producing no feeling of nausea. She began to glide along the winding river, never going really high apart from one moment when she climbed above buzzing power cables, only to drop back down again.

In places the river gets more overgrown as you go upstream, to disappear for a while in piping as it flows under the town. On the other side, after crossing fields, it goes into much wilder country, the ground too steep or uneven to be broken by the plough in the past and just left wild.

'It is normally now, here, has been in the past, she likes here' thought Typos. Pushing my memory, I can remember getting increasingly intrigued. I was on the point of asking who or what this was all about when up ahead on a wide bend in the river by the side of a large pool, I saw a woman. Even from a height, I could see that she was clad in a long brown dress which touched the ground. Her hair was very long and bleached blonde by the sun. Something sparkled around her neck, and she turned and walked out of sight under a large oak. To my utter incredulity she then reappeared by the water's edge. She looked up to us and lifted a hand in welcome.

'She can see you' I thought to Typos.

'I hope so' came the answer in a slightly sarcastic tone. Gliding down, she started looking for a place big enough to land. After her usual dramatic landing amid showers of grass, she ruffled her wings, and after shaking them, turned her head back to me.

'The time is now, back again, real... you can get off and meet.'

'Yes, but who is she?'

'Too small for me to go in, I wait hereabouts watching for you.' Now you can imagine the astonishment I felt as she added, 'She is the goddess Freyja, friend of Acionna the water goddess, here now from afar. Give her respect, she wants to meet you. Go!'

I wriggled until I fell off to her side.

'A goddess, how can that be? They are folklore, mythology...'

'She is real.'

'Promise you will be here' I urged her, looking straight into her eyes.

'You are safe, wanted, have no fear, go! I watch and wait.' She was smiling now. 'Her tongue is not yours, my mother knew her, from a far land.' She paused as if allowing me to absorb these strange thoughts.

'That makes her old, but she is not. Even from a distance I could see that. You have got that wrong surely?'

'No, that is right. You meet her and you see, age is your concept, not hers or mine. She is not you. I watch from here. Go!'

She was almost ordering me now, and if she had been human I am sure she would have given me a push. I turned and started walking to the pool, having to raise my arms to go through a big patch of red-hot nettles which tried to sting my legs. On the other side grass began, and the poolside was calm. Sunlight twinkled through, bracken grew on the far edge, and in the trees woodpigeons were cooing 'Johnny no jam' repeatedly. All was warm and very calming.

'Hello' I called out. 'You wanted to meet me, I have been told.'

No answer came back, and I was about to call out again, but from the far pool side I heard a gentle splash and a head surfaced through the water. Long, wet, shiny blonde hair framed the most beautiful face I had ever seen. She was smiling at me, with teeth even and unnaturally white. She swam across to me in a few strokes. As she reached the edge she put her feet down and raised herself from of the water. I saw that around her neck was the most beautiful necklace. It was heavy, a silver and gold chain carrying beautifully carved stones of amber. It held my attention fully, shining in the sun, the most exquisite thing I had ever seen, delicate and natural, an example of great beauty.

I tore my eyes away from it to look up at her face and saw her looking directly at me, smiling at my wonderment. Her eyes held me and seemed to be probing my mind. I realised that in front of me was the most beautiful woman I had ever seen. My heart was racing.

And then as she left the water, I realised that she was completely naked. The water was running down and over the curves of her body.

'I am so sorry, please forgive me. I had no idea,' I mumbled hopelessly, looking at the ground. I could feel my face redden.

I felt her hands touch my shoulders. 'It is fine, if you worry, wait' she said. I heard her go to the side of the clearing and then, 'You can turn, it is fine'. Her accent was vaguely Norwegian or perhaps

Swedish, and her speech was broken as she found the words. I turned around.

She stood by the water's edge smiling at me, her eyes twinkling and a smile filling her face. At her feet, winding themselves in and out of her legs, were two jet-black cats. Their coats shone as if they were made of glass, and I could hear them purring. On the other side of the pool another cat sat staring at me.

'I am Freyja and you are Myrddin, a watcher for man,' she said.

Well, what could I say other than 'Hello, it is nice to meet you'? I admit that I was hopelessly out of my depth. I was entranced by this lady. I look around, and for want of hiding my discomfort, kicked liked an embarrassed schoolboy at a dock near my feet. I was lost. I grinned back at her like an idiot, feeling at a complete loss for words.

She smiled and beckoned me to her. 'I asked Typos to meet, felt the moment, that is how' she said. Her accent was soft, almost musical, and I was about to say how long I had been with Typos when her right hand went up and settled, holding her necklace. I looked at it again, entranced. It was so achingly beautiful, just as she was.

'This is Brisingamen I wear, my torc, do you say necklace? Made by dwarves and elves.' She paused for a moment. 'I paid a price for it.' She stopped, lost for a moment in thought. As she said this I was alarmed to see her eyes momentarily fill with tears. One rolled down her check and I was truly stunned as I followed its course until it fell on the ground glistening like gold in the half light at her feet. She absent-minded pulled at the necklace, moving it up and down and pulling it around her neck with both hands.

'It is lovely, how can you risk getting it wet?' I paused, looking at her. 'Is everything all right? Can I help?'

This was all I could say. I really wanted to go over and comfort her, for the sorrow on her face was obviously real. She turned her eyes back to me, and the sorrow left her face. She smiled so intensely that I found myself smiling back. In a moment we both started giggling and then, for no real reason, we both burst into laughter.

She came over to me, taking my hands and pulling me over to the base of the oak, and lifted a bottle from the ground, a leather bottle with a wood stopper. This she pulled out, and she put the bottle to her lips.

'Here now for you. It is good!'

Without asking what it was - she was not likely to be drinking poison, I thought - I put the rough bottle to my mouth. The taste was like honey and whisky together, hinting at orange. It was delicious, and without thinking I drank some more.

She started to laugh and reached up to take the bottle back, its contents audibly sloshing. 'Enough, that is all, it works' she said. She looked across at me, her smile perfect. This attractive vision had hooked me, and I had no resistance.

We went across to the sunny edge and sat down. The woodpigeons carried on murmuring and a faint noise from the stream filled the air. Her cats lolled in a sunny patch and then wandered off.

Our conversation remained stilted at first, but gradually it grew easier.

'I have watched you with Acionna's followers each year.' She paused, seeing the question forming on my face.

'You witness her support for the water, for humans here. Your followers do the same all over the world. It is good, ancient and necessary.'

'The river lights that dance?' I whispered back.

'Yes those, it has been for ages, since the beginning.'

'This year my new follower, the next Merlin... when I am gone...' I started to say.

'I know, we watched.' She put her hand on my arm and gave it a squeeze. 'You are never alone!' She started to laugh, and pointed at my face. 'Don't look so worried, you are part of an ancient order, chosen, I remember well.'

Now I have to admit to having been a bit lost in thought at this point. This woman appeared to be about my age, achingly pretty, and yet, saying that she knew my choosing. Typos had said she knew her, her mother had as well.

At this time of our first meeting I was well into my thirty-ninth year. It just did not add up. She was too young-looking. Something was wrong, and I was worried.

Our conversation went on, the afternoon sun began to go down and the dusk chorus from the bushes began as birds tuned up.

'I'd better think of going' I said, not really wanting to. I looked sadly at her.

'We will meet again soon, Typos will do. She can always find me, it is a must.' Freyja smiled at me and then her face became serious. 'Do you say... please? We meet soon?'

The intensity of this, to be honest, matched my own feelings.

'Yes of course, I am sure.' I struggled to my feet, momentarily losing my balance and clutching inadvertently at her.

She turned her head up to me, smiled and kissed me gently on the lips.

'We must meet soon.'

I walked back out of the clearing, stopping to turn and half wave. She waved back and I heard her giggle.

Typos was waiting outside on the wood edge, and as I climbed clumsily onto her neck her mind joined mine and dragged every memory out.

'She is nice then.'

'Yes very nice, very very nice' I jokily thought back, and then laughed in happiness as we flew back.

I almost forgot to tell you that before leaving, Typos climbed back up above the small pool. Freyja was not in sight, but in the middle of the clearing, in the fading sunlight, a red fallow deer stood, just looking up at us.

* * *

I did not sleep at all easily for the next few weeks, but then as I was walking across the hill above my house one miserable gloomy damp morning, Typos appeared again.

'Watch out, someone will see you' I thought to her in panic, looking around.

'You must call me, you always used to, crikey, look around quick!'

Her relaxed answer gave me some relief. 'It is fine, no one, I have checked, but you are needed.'

I must admit that my excited reply gave me away.

'What, by Freyja?'

Not wanting to hear any other answer, I was thrilled by her laid-back reply.

'Correct, but we go a distance, this morning is good. It is how you say... misty though. Difficult to find, maybe.'

I crossed over to her, giving her neck my usual big hug, which somehow I have realised she likes. With me settled we were airborne, but soon the ground was lost through the fog layer. It was very patchy as we flew on, with big gaps allowing the odd house to show, a very distinct layer as up above it a weak sun shone.

I must admit to losing my bearings somewhat and was really surprised to see through the now thinning mist the main road to our nearest town.

'She waits near the hill here, on the wild side. I will go down soon.'

'I know where we are now, how will you know where she is?'

'We will see her, it is no problem here.'

A moment later I looked down to see an enormous black boar. As it ambled along, it turned its head up to look at us. Its great body rippled with massive muscles, and its pelt rippled with each step. As it turned its great head up its long tusks showed, brown and fearsome. Wild boar are not that unusual around here, but they normally stay in the upland woods, and this one was bigger than any I had seen before. It was making its way along very purposefully. It looked up at us, and carried on walking.

'That is Hildisvini, he is always with her' thought Typos to me.

'Hang on, do you mean that boar down there - that is hers?'

'Not hers. With her, with her, do you say, cats.'

To say that I was stunned at this casual remark would be an understatement.

'She has... animals with her?'

'You will see. Wrong words. They are her - do you say – workmates.'

At this point I remained quiet, and shall we say somewhat bemused, and then Typos flared down into a narrow ghyll, shrouded by a clump of gorse on one side and the remains of an old stone barn.

'Go, she will wait by that wall for you. I will wait. All is safe.'

'Right I'll do that' I whispered back, still confused.

Wriggling down onto the sheep-cropped grass, walking up to the barn remains, I suppose for reassurance, I looked back at Typos, who unbelievably seemed to have her eyes shut, sleeping. Over the valley below us the mist and fog began to roll in, and nearing the barn, I was so pleased to see Freyja. She had her long brown dress on, the one I had seen her in before, the lovely Brisingamen necklace shone at her open neck, the gold and amber set against her milky skin. Over her shoulders was draped a cloak that made faint rustling noises as she moved towards me. As she got nearer I could see that it was made of hundreds of feathers, all aligned and hanging down, looking almost as if they grew out of her. Her face was beaming in a massive smile, her teeth strikingly white, her skin soft, with a slight tan. Her chalky blue eyes twinkled and her long, long blonde hair hung down loose.

I did not know what to say. I had started to mumble when I realised that at my feet, rubbing against my leg, were her three cats. I laughed out loud and bent down, then squatted to greet them and stroke them.

'Hello, you lot, you again, do you remember me?' I said. I laughed again as with backs arched they patrolled around in front of me.

'They know and recall' said Freyja, walking to me with her arms outstretched. She walked up to me, put her hands on my shoulders, reached up to me and kissed me gently.

'Hello again. I spoke to Typos. She brought you as I asked.'

'You can talk to Typos?' I answered, stunned.

She smiled. 'Do not be surprised, I spoke to her mother often.'

'Now hang on a moment.' I lifted one hand and looked at her, smiling. 'Look, I don't want to be rude, but how can you have known her mother? To be honest I still miss her. Typos is wonderful, but I shared so much with Shola. It's tricky - Typos is really for Will, the next Myrddin.'

She looked away from me, then out across the valley, not saying anything, making me feel momentarily worried.

'It is not of your now' she turned and said to me. 'Typos has told you I am different.' She lifted a hand to stop me as I was about to speak.

'It is now, I talk to you. You have a right to know, but you are different too.'

She looked back at me, walked back and taking my hand, pulled me gently over to the wall. Stopping in front of it, she unclipped her cloak and spread it on the ground.

'We can sit' she said, smiling up at me and gesturing at the cloak. We both settled down, side by side, and the cold from the ground was lost. The cloak had a light lining of a line-like material, and individual feathers could be felt under it. I was painfully aware that my heavy boots might somehow damage it, and reached down to loosen and pull them off.

'It is strong, you will not break it' she said, turning to look at me. From her side she pulled another leather bottle, smaller than the last. Pulling out the stopper, she put it to her lips. After a sip she passed it to me, but kept a firm hand on it. I looked at her questioningly.

'Only a little' she ordered, using a sharper tone. 'This is different, Typos knows and agrees. This is to help you know about me. It will open, do you say, your mind? Then it will go.'

'I do not do drugs' I said back, half laughing.

'It is the same as you had by the water with me, but more do you say... working?'

'You will have me becoming an alcoholic' I joked back.

'What is alcoholic?'

'Alcoholic - don't worry I am joking. Here give it to me.' I reached out for it. Smiling back she passed it to me, and thinking 'in for a penny, in for a pound', I took a big gulp, and then before she could react, another.

'There, very nice' I laughed, giving it back, as she, with a worried look, bade me lie down. Thinking back with hindsight, did I feel drunk? No, not really. Receptive, yes. It did work not right away, but I felt my eyes wanting to close.

As they shut I was aware of Freyja lying down beside me, putting her arm across my chest and whispering in my ear. All felt right in the world. I was warm, comfortable and I had this beautiful woman lying by me. In my sleepy state, I realised that Freyja was, as Typos had explained, a goddess from the north.

You will by now be thinking, this is weird, rubbish! But in my sleepy, hypnotic state it made gentle sense, and since then all has been reassuringly confirmed to me. This woman I have learnt to love, and she me.

That morning she explained that she had a brother, Freyr, and she had originally lived in her hall, Sessrumnir, which stood in Folkvangr, a town in Asgard, the realm of the gods. With her brother and her father, Njoror, they had called Shola often, hence the connection.

I should say that she made no mention of her mother, nor has she since, despite my gentle hints to her. And when I asked about husbands, men in her life, she would not tell me. In fact later, to my horror and sadness, such questions produced head shaking, looking at the floor, away from me, and as before tears, which seemed to turn to liquid gold on touching the ground.

In my sleepy state she cuddled closer to me, and as I roused I could feel her warmth.

'Hello' I sleepily mumbled back as she kissed me very gently. I stretched my legs out, feeling warm and very relaxed.

'You now know some of me' she smilingly said, propping her head on both hands and looking down at me. Her eyes twinkled.

'There is a lot of you to know' I said, reaching out to touch her face.

'We have time' was her reply.

'But I do not, I am human, not a god. And in any case I have just eighty-five years as Myrddin, then I finish.'

She smiled and replied, 'Not so. As reward you get another... Typos when it is right will arrange, will tell. You could be with me.'

'With you? Are you being serious?'

The thought of that, both then and now, has driven me on.

At that time another mass of misty cloud rolled in on us, cold and wet. She had just wriggled even tighter to me when out of the corner of my eye, I saw the great hairy shape of the boar arrive. It snorted as it came up to us.

'Quick, get behind me' I shouted, struggling to my feet. She laughed and pointed at me.

'It is not funny, they can be dangerous, quick behind me, please, please!'

She smiled and waved both hands in a calming gesture. 'He is mine. Hildisvine is always near and with me. It is fine!'

The boar wandered over to her, pushing his great head forward for her to tickle. He then turned to look at me, with nothing but contempt in its tiny eyes. He turned back to her, bowed his great head and with a last derisory glance at me, wandered off, up the hill and into the mist.

Getting to her feet, she walked over to me and gave me a tight hug.

'He is always with me, you will see him many times. He is fine!'

'Well, they have been known to kill men I believe, certainly dogs. They are strong and dangerous.'

She smiled up at me.

'We will meet again soon, many times Typos will bring you. You are mine and I am your future.' She stood on tiptoe and kissed me. 'Your friend is at risk of being seen, we have next time, keep her safe.'

To my amazement she called Typos, to be answered not audibly but mentally, as with me. I looked at her stunned, and laughed.

'You as well! Do I have no secrets?'

'No, none. You are mine Myrddin. Be safe until next time.' She pulled me to her, kissing me again. 'Go on, go now, our time will come.'

I walked down the hill to find Typos. She did not think anything to me, but bent her great head down with an odd expression on her face. If she had been human she would have had one eyebrow raised questioningly.

'All well,' she eventually thought as I wriggled into my place on her neck, between her spines.

'Oh very well, very well,' I thought back. 'Come on, do something wild, I am excited.'

'My mother told me you liked this, well, we go. Sit tight, but I will catch if you fall.'

With an enormous bound we were airborne. She flew off at breakneck speed, soaring high over the Channel, to drop like a stone almost to the waves. I whooped with joy, feeling all was right in my world. As indeed it was.

CHAPTER 9

THE CHALLENGE OF THE WIND FURIES

Always as Christmas approached I became a little anxious and easily irritated, knowing that the Wind Furies would call for their meeting.

One miserable afternoon in late autumn, Will and I sat by the Aga putting the world to rights. Outside it had done nothing but rain, for days it seemed. The horses were in early, their sopping wet New Zealands off, pulling at their hay nets.

Settled early for the night, the bored dogs wandered in and out of the kitchen, making a tour of the house; now and then in a dejected manner they would scrap with each other. It had been so vile that trips outside with me just meant checking sheep, fiddling with horses and mucking out. The shooting season would start in earnest soon, and perhaps, if it got crisp and cold, sanity would return to me and to the dogs.

'Go on, have another bit of cake' I said, shoving a plate along the counter top. 'Look I need to fill you in about something sad about Typos and her mum. She has already told me that you will be called, with me, to see these wretched Wind Furies that she has to meet each year.'

His mouth stuffed with cake, he nodded at me. 'What do you mean, sad?' he asked, looking concerned.

'It was a while ago, in fact years, but for her it's still very real. If you ever think to her about it... well, don't, avoid it.'

Clutching my mug of tea, I explained gently to him that every year, usually about now, they would call, first with her mother then Typos, to meet. She never knew where or when until just before.

'Negotiations some years were easy but there have been a few when they were horrible. They seemed to relish her having to see the horrors that she and her mother had tried to modify.' I lifted my hand, adding, 'It is not always that bad. There were good things they did for her as well. They helped Shola with the defeat of the Spanish Armada, centuries ago.'

I paused to sip some tea, looking at him.

'Anyway, one year for some reason, goodness knows why, they got stroppy with her mother, and when she twitched back they arranged for her to be blown into some power cables. She threw me off deliberately to save me, but she perished horribly, in the wires. I ended up in hospital. It's a long story, as you can probably imagine. It took a while before I could meet Typos again, and on one occasion she and her friends went to meet the furies. Well, there was a fight to avenge her mother. Typos is still very sensitive about this. Sadly, every year since then she has been saying how she felt the furies gain strength.'

At this point I looked at him. 'She says that man is making the seas warmer, the melting ice caps being a sign, but their strength increases each year. We are nothing but the human witnesses to this, but I already feel it is getting to be a problem again. Anyway, enough said. We will have to wait and see. You are getting the hang of everything, I know. We will be meeting the other watchers in a few weeks, I will take care of you, it is a bit of a trip. I'll have to teach you how to apply extra power, and we can do a bit of animal talk. Jules had a thing called 'shape shifting' and I will go through it with you.

'I have to be honest, some of the force things he taught me I have never used – they made me feel dreadful - but they have been developed by our predecessors, so they need to be kept together. Make no mistake, there is lots to know, and well... I suppose lots of responsibility. Great eh, just what you needed!

'You have seen the Beltane with the spring waking lady, the river forces or fairies.'

I smiled at this point. Will looked up at me, biting his lip and said 'Yes, but are the dragon calls always as ghastly as the first one? That was horrible seeing all that death, and those truly awful demons trying to take souls... I hated that.'

I looked at him, and it was obvious that it had taken a lot of bottle to say what he had. I thought long and hard before answering.

'To be honest with you, I suppose on thinking about it, most calls from her have been to witness some horror she has to sort. At my beginnings I had to see her mother dealing with plague pits near here, and be on alert for an eclipse. But you know Shola helped Jules with a terminally-ill boy, and arrived to help fire the Torrey Canyon oil spill as well.

'Also - wait a minute - I remember Jules telling me that Shola helped a knight out - St. George, in fact. You see, it is very varied. Typos helped me to return an abducted child a few years ago.' I looked intently at him. 'It does not happen often, sometimes not for months, but you are very privileged to be the one who represents human presence. You are going to meet the Wind Furies soon, for sure. You now have Typos as your best mate, and you can talk to dogs and of course horses. What else?'

I looked at him and smiled. 'All that medicinal herb stuff we have gone through time and again, if you can remember it.'

He looked at the floor, and I knew he was dreading me asking him more questions about homeopathy and the herbs, questions we had covered time and again over the past eighteen months.

'I know how to call Typos and when not to, but tell me, what do you do when she calls you and you just cannot answer?' he asked. 'Apart from throw up, that is.' He laughed.

I paused, not wanting to make it too heavy for him, and watched his reaction.

'It has never ever been a problem, I promise' I answered. 'But you will need to do it by yourself soon. Just call her to a private place, where you cannot be seen. The next time I see her I will tell her you are going to. It is a big thing I know, but you will manage, don't worry.'

I paused to let the dogs out into the garden. In the usual way they were convinced that there were bad men out there who needed woofing at and sorting out. Peace returned once they had gone.

'Anyway, sometimes she does not call for months and I can remember having to call her a few times.'

'Another cup?' I said, looking.

'Yes thanks' he replied, passing his mug to me.

'Soon she will call to see the Wind Furies and yes, one week after the shortest day this year we get, well... ratified. Permission, if you like, with the other watchers. They are a nice bunch, you will like them. I will take you this time, but it may not be possible for me the next.'

'What on earth do you mean, going abroad or something?' he joked, shuffling on his stool.

'Well, you never know.' I could hardly tell him that I was going to die.

I do not mind telling you as I write that the thought of being dead did not worry me a jot. Of course it would be sad, but Typos had plans which Freyja has confirmed many times.

Eventually, as darkness dropped, Will said cheerio to us all, pulled his skid-lid on, fired up his scooter and rode off, leaving behind that distinctive-smelling blue cloud of two stroke exhaust.

* * *

Only two days after that, I was reaching down a string of onions when Typos called. I can remember that it was so intense that I nearly lost my balance on the chair I was using to reach them.

I shut all the house windows, settled the horses and dogs and found my heavy waterproof and gloves. The dogs all got up from their beds and stood at the door, wagging their tails, all set for their normal ambush.

'Got her call then, you made good time, well done,' I called out to Will through the glass as he walked up to the back door.

'I was coming along here anyway. I nearly fell into the ditch when it came!' He had started unbuttoning his coat and was coming through the door after the doggie welcome.

'Yes but you didn't, well done. Leave everything on.'

We left the house, walking as quickly as I could across the hill to the barn. It was already getting colder, with a hint of the sun going. Heavy clouds were forming out at sea and being driven in by a strengthening wind.

'The sky's looking odd' said Will, nodding upwards.

'It's certainly changing, and it's started going wrong in the last hour, I suppose. Anyway come on, tell you what, she is your call today. I'll be beside you, don't worry. Keep it slow and precise, like I have told you. Go on, it's a doddle!' I smiled at him.

He looked back at me, half smiling, then walked over to the barn.

'All right, but only if you listen and tell me off if it's wrong.'

I laughed. 'Go on, you'll be fine. Just don't rush, it gathers its own speed. I have always supposed it is as she hears and prepares to come.'

'Over here as normal?' said Will, and I nodded back. We settled, kneeling down and I waited. There was silence.

'I'm so sorry, like a Charlie I have completely forgot the start.' said Will. He looked embarrassed. I opened my eyes, and smiled, telling him it was just nerves. When I whispered the opening words, he looked aghast.

'Of course, how could I forget? It's all right now.'

The rest of his attempt was fine. Typos was in front of us more quickly than usual, and I could see straight away that she was in a high state of alert. She was erect, straight-legged and ready to spring. Her head was held upright, and her eyes when she looked at me were hard, wolf-like, full of intent. Her muscles visibly rippled under her skin, which seemed to have much more shine than usual. In fact when I got nearer the sheen of sweat was obvious, and that distinct smell of leather and lemon was hanging in the air.

She was obviously wound up about something and every breath, it seemed, was accompanied by a flame from her mouth, which varied from a small flicker to a frightening blast. With one of these I saw out of the corner of my eye that Will was shrinking back, looking petrified and flinging his hands up to his face.

'Fine' I mouthed at him, lifting my hand. I turned to Typos. 'What is wrong, do you have a problem? A worry?'

She turned to look down at me, and I reassuringly felt her join.

'As I have been waiting, they call,' she said. At the word 'call', a massive flame shot from her upturned head, going on for many seconds.

'They have a plan. I am being helped by friends in case... they do not know.'

At this point I wished I had explained to Will in a bit more detail the last dragon event.

'We go, on! We go to, how do you say - North, Scottish land to wait. That is their call.'

I checked Will had done his coat up and we got settled on her neck. With us snug, without any further thought she sprung airborne, a massive leap that took our breath away. Then she thought to us, 'We go, to your start of this century, to your year one nine five three.' With this she twitched out. The seasonal landscape below us had hardly changed.

'We are just back a few years, you feel OK Will?' I hissed into

Will's ear, against a headwind which hammered in to us, bringing stinging rain. He nodded back, half turning to me, not saying anything.

Below us it was getting murkier and murkier. The wind was shifting a little with height so that now it met us on Typos' left side. With height it decreased and mercifully the rain eased off. Typos' broad wings seemed to chew at the distance, as she flew purposefully on.

Soon, to my amazement, the lights of Bristol came below us. The Severn estuary looked jet black, with the city itself lit up. The floodlit roads coming in to it looked like arteries.

I pushed Will gently in the back. 'Look, below to the right, a plane taking off from the airport. Look at its propellers, don't see that often now.'

Just a few powerful wing beats later, the gentle hills of Wales showed through the murk on our left. At this point Will, who had shrunk into his coat, flung his hands over his ears as full-volume dragon speak filled our heads.

'She is here' thought Typos to us. 'My friend Y Draig Goch.'

The shiver could be felt through her back. She was ecstatic, almost as if she could be singing. Will turned to me and mouthed 'what?

'It is one of her friends' I said. I now remembered this dragon from years before.

At that very moment, above us, she glided down and then, with wings working much faster, another dragon joined us. I looked across and then back to Will. He was looking with staring eyes, mouth open, his gaze fixed.

'Another dragon? No!' He was stunned.

'Yes, forget all your teachers, all those books you thought were real, this is real and it's happening now. You will see lots of strange things, and Typos is not the only one. Get real Will! This is for now, for you and me, what luck eh, to have such mates!'

The other dragon came noisily alongside, its wings making a faint whistling noise as they beat. She did not seem to glide at all. Her wings were perpetually beating fast, never stopping. She was meat-red all over and her neck carried whitened patches that looked like old healed injuries. Her sharply-taloned back legs dangled behind her, seeming to move to and fro with her wing beats. She had a long neck extended in front, which supported a snake-like head which as I looked turned to me. The eyes were unreceptive and cold, devoid of passion. It was a frightening stare which showed utter contempt. I quickly turned away, and Will did the same.

A kind of conversation began between the dragons, but it was way beyond us. It was apparent that the dragons were catching up with each other's news.

The pair flew along at a leisurely pace, the rain returning and the wind noticeably increasing in strength. Now and then great gusts slammed in to us, forcing us to grab a firmer hold. Now and then it seemed almost as if there were holes in the air. We would drop, producing a transient feeling of nausea.

The dragons sculled along without an apparent care in the world. Will and I just sat tight waiting, the occasional light from towns below us showing our progress.

'She comes' Typos thought, disturbing our personal thoughts. 'You will remember her, not fully like us, but good friend.'

'Do you mean it is…?'

'Yes, it is Heptaco, here we are complete. We begin.'

I could feel Will's amazement; he was speechless. With his head turned high to the right, he watched the new dragon's arrival.

I remembered Heptaco from the time before. She was, or is, not a dragon at all but a wyvern. Tiny front legs could just be made out, but the biggest difference was the way she hardly moved her wings. Shorter and stubbier than normal dragon wings, they were beating almost constantly. She was predominantly blue and green above her wings, and as she rolled in the wind I saw that she was a speckled brownish-green underneath. She was much smaller than the others, and as she caught my stare I was held by her tiny, pig-like eyes.

'We will deal now, we meet, it is not expected' thought Typos to us, her attitude changed. All three dragons formed a line across, and without any prompting or apparent command, they issued long fiery blasts. The gloomy day was lit with the glow of fire, and there was a smell as of fireworks.

Through the now worsening weather and failing light we flew on, until, it seemed ages later, we heard Typos again.

'We go down, leave you here to watch, wait, on that low hill.'

The other two stayed circling above as Typos, with a face shaking drop, shot down to a hill.

'Off now, until later when I return' she said. With her now almost compulsory shower of peat and heather she flared to land. We both wriggled off, and stood by her.

'Look be careful, no harm allowed' I stressed, feeling that I wanted to hold and shake her to emphasize the point. 'This has got memories of times before. We will wait, but do not be long, we will worry,' I admitted.

Typos was obviously a bit distracted but she did turn, and I swear she smiled at me. 'They want now, my duty to them, the usual… they have plan which we will modify for better. I am not alone, we see.'

With that, her great back legs audibly creaking with effort, she sprang up. Her open wings gave a massive thrust which almost pushed us over.

We both stood quietly watching her go off into the gloom. Both of us pulled our jacket collars up and Will pulled his hands up inside his sleeves. The cold and wet was very real now that we had lost Typos' body warmth.

'Come on, let's duck below that wall over there, it's a tad parky,' I joked.

'We will want to watch the sky where they are, surely?' said Will, looking across at me. He started to walk back across the hill top to the wall.

'Yes for sure, but they could take hours yet, who knows.'

We walked in and looked out at the sea, just visible as silvery streaks a long way below us. We hunkered down, using the stones of the wall as a shelter and backrest. We were not yet too cold, but we were getting wetter and the wind was noticeably increasing.

Within I suppose no more than half an hour, the wind became alarming. To stand on our hill top was becoming virtually impossible, and out to sea the sky began to be fissured by lightning. Soon the thunderous peals moved in, and up above us the sky was lit by savage forks of lightning. A great deluge accompanied it. However the wind speed kept gusting to gale force, so we both had to lie almost flat to resist it. Speech was impossible at anything below shouting volume, and the clouds above hammered along, driven inland by the gale.

Thinking back, it is strange what you remember, but I have to tell you that I was really glad that in my pocket was a bag of the trusty pineapple chunks. I offered them to a surprised Will. In fact they kept us going as the wind carried on increasing, howling ever louder around us, until early the next morning, when our jackets were beginning to give up the job. As usual the shoulder seams failed first, and soon our backs were soaked.

At last it began to lull a little, making conversation possible.

'When are they back then, normally?' asked Will, the worry obvious in his voice.

'Oh, it could be a while yet.' I tried to appear nonchalant, but inwardly I always worry dreadfully at this point in the year. To try and fill his knowledge in a bit and reassure him, I said, 'This is a strange call for her, I always feel we're a bit redundant. Still, here we are. One year when I was just starting with Jules, we went with Shola to witness a horrific storm that caused immense coastal damage. People were killed, and afterwards she was so tired she could hardly fly us back. She crashed out in the barn, and we had to hide her under a load of hay. It seems funny, looking back on it, but at the time it was ghastly.'

Now I am going to interrupt to say that it was only at times like this that I realised just how fond of this great, wonderful lump I was. To my surprise and inward delight I could hear in Will's voice that he was hooked by her spell as well.

The wind dropped down again as that wonderful voice we had both been waiting for called in our heads. We both looked at each other and smiled, big beaming smiles.

Through the drizzle Typos appeared. She collapsed on the ground, her flanks moving up and down, her mouth wide open, sucking in air. Will stood dumbfounded at this sight, and turned to look at me, just as Heptaco the wyvern appeared and collapsed alongside her.

'What can we do?' shouted Will to me, as he ran over to them both.

'Give their legs room, for goodness sake!' I shouted back. 'All we can do is wait for them to recover. Thankfully they are out of sight, but go quickly down that path and stop anyone coming up, I don't care how. Go, go on!'

I pointed down the track and he took one glance at me and hared off.

I went over to Typos and knelt down by her head. Her eyes flickered open.

'What have you done, you lovable brute?' I said as I lifted the great head, with difficulty, to cradle it in my arms. Her breathing was starting to calm down, her mouth shut, but her nostrils were flaring with each fall of her flanks.

'I will be fine, just tired, so tired.'

'You are safe, sleep' I thought back. 'We will watch, all is safe. Is Heptaco well?' Then it occurred to me. 'What about Y Draig Goch, where is she?'

I had no answer. Sleep descended upon Typos like a solid blanket. My legs were jammed under her increasingly heavy head, and I looked over at the unconscious wyvern. I could just make out her breathing, and now and then involuntary convulsions racked her body.

The morning sun began to clear the night away, and carefully I moved first one leg and then the other from under her head. A fair amount of cursing later, I was standing and pulling at my sodden clothes. I looked at the two of them, sparked out.

I wondered if Will was OK, and started walking a little way down the path. I was relieved at seeing him below me, a tiny dot amongst the heather. He lifted one hand with a thumb up, a gesture which I returned. Then, with him watching, I mimed a keep-fit exercise, jumping up and down on the spot and windmilling my arms. Even from that distance I heard a laugh and saw him start warming up.

I wandered back to the top, alternating between close observation, worry, listening to make sure of breathing, and immense concern. Possibly four hours passed. Then, to my dismay, a gasping Will arrived, hardly able to speak. He grabbed me by the shoulder, and turned and pointed over the rise.

'Walkers or climbers are coming! Only perhaps an hour and a half below us. What are we going to do? There's a party of them, about twenty I should think.'

'Did they see you?' I asked, grabbing his shoulders.

'Possibly, I have no idea.'

'Never mind, it was bound to happen. These two are done in, but they have to wake and go. Come on.'

We walked over to Typos first. She was making faint snoring noises. I really had no idea what to do, but I began calling her audibly and mentally. Will joined in, and at the same time I started rubbing her head, pulling her great ear and scratching around her ear canal. Her eyelid began to flicker, and the snoring stopped. We called louder, and eventually all four legs were stretched. There were loud groans, a thunderous fart and she was awake.

We were so pleased to see her like this that both Will and I gave her great head and scaly neck a big hug.

'We have not long, people are coming, we have not woken Heptaco yet' I thought to her. 'It is tight, come on, not long.'

Both Will and I shot to the side as she got to her four legs and lifted her wings up and away from her body with much groaning. Typos eventually went over to the wyvern and roughly shook her with one retracted talon repeatedly until she roused. Heptaco, with a great rush, was awake and ready. She sprang to her feet, looking around. I rushed over.

'Typos, please thank her for all she did, not just for us, but all, please?'

'That is done, they were contained, though not fully. It was good. Your thanks are good. She goes.'

With those last words the wyvern looked slowly around at Will and me, the small pig-like eyes showing little emotion, but you could almost imagine a smile. With a snatch of final dragon talk between them, the wyvern ran to the hill edge, slowly becoming airborne. Then she twitched out and was gone.

'Now you two, on we go, the sun comes higher.'

Almost as soon as we were safe on her neck, Typos twitched back. In the early morning light the flight back was clear. She was too tired to go high, and soon our barn was alongside us. We both slid to the ground and walked around to her head.

'Before you ask, Y Draig Goch was hurt and went back early, but she will be fine' she told us. What could I think to her but 'Our wishes for a speedy recovery, and give us our thanks'. I know what you're thinking, but what else could I say? Anyway these characters are tough, and I have come to appreciate that they actually like confrontation.

'Typos, you have to go, we are aware, but what happened? What did you have to do?'

Will and I stood in stunned silence as she explained that the furies had arranged a massive storm, trying to lay waste to great swathes of the British Isles. The dragons had been only partially successful, but they had managed to restrict the damage.

For what it's worth, I repeat that at one point Typos fixed me with a stern look and said, 'man is making their forces stronger, something is changing, they are getting stronger, the wheals on this land, sea and air get deeper, they break!'

With a last look at both of us, a very tired Typos bid her goodbye, and with Will and me both watching she twitched out and was gone, leaving us to walk back to the dogs and a big fried breakfast.

* * *

For the doubtful or the questioner, go to your history books. On the first of February 1953 a violent storm arrived, northerly winds lashing the country, with torrential rain breaking down flood defences. The mayhem started in Ireland, passing over Scotland and then out over the North Sea. On the East coast the combination of rising tides and high winds meant thousands of homes were flooded, claiming hundreds of lives. The official figures said that 307 British people were killed and over 20,000 homes were flooded, with 30,000 left homeless. Many tens of thousands of animals were killed.

Without sounding too obvious, just imagine how much worse it would have been if we had not had those three dragons trying to fight our corner.

Typos was becoming aware then of how man was changing his planet; I will not be around to do much about it, but you will. For the sake of the future, I urge you to take action now to stop all the pollution.

CHAPTER 10

THE WATCHERS AT THE STONES

The rain splattered on the windscreen as I rather dejectedly looked out. I had been sitting in the car in the yard now for about ten minutes waiting for Will. He was never late, always early, so this was out of character.

Both horses suddenly appeared at the stable doors and whickered a welcome as the scooter arrived, belching its usual fumes. I wound the window down as he parked up, wrestled his 'lid' off and dropped it in the feed room. He came almost jogging back, lifted a hand in welcome and waved for me to go out of the yard onto the road so he could shut the main gates. Once on the road he opened the door, flung himself in and grabbed his seat belt. He turned to look at me, smiling.

'What a trip! Bit later than I promised, the road by the Tunnel is blocked. I had to go around.'

'No worries, we have plenty of time, but it's a bit of a trek. You'll have to get an old banger for next year.'

'Or go with you again' he answered.

I turned to say something, but then thought better of it. The rain was getting heavier, and a few oncoming cars had put their lights on. I glanced over at Will.

'You know it is strange, but I have been going to these for fifty-odd years now. Although it can be chucking it down, snowing or freezing, the evening always becomes dry, almost barmy. It always has, never fails to be nice.'

The traffic was not too heavy as we made our way over to the main trunk road for London. The car radio kept us going and we made general chitchat whilst shoving in my pineapple chunks - the sweets, I suppose, I was famous for. I always had them with me in some pocket or other. I found Will getting a bag of them out of his pocket the other day. He has great taste!

The main road was flowing freely as usual, and once on it we made good progress, driving past the Naval Air Station as two helicopters left, chewing noisily into the air.

'We have it easier with Typos' said Will, pointing to them.

'Dead right, many years ago Shola virtually flew me over here, it was really neat looking down on them. Great machines, aren't they?'

The rain had eased down to the odd splattering, with the car wipers just having to cope with road spray. Soon the road carves through open country and on each side massive tractors could be seen turning the soil, breaking up the remaining old stubble.

'Look, this thing tonight,' I started saying to Will, reaching down to turn down the radio. 'It has happened every year here for, well for ever, I suppose. I missed a few following my accident with Shola, and my absence caused great problems for them all. It is now back to normal, has been for years but... look, somehow you have just got to ensure you make it.' I threw a quick glance at him.

'Somehow, the countries of Ireland, Wales and Scotland all have a watcher. And no, I am still not sure how they choose their follower, but over the years they have individually brought their replacements along. Always the year before they die.'

I stopped talking to deal with the wiper blades, as the rain increased again and the traffic all slowed to a snail's pace.

'I get the suspicion they know we are different. One of them, I think it was Wales, caught me out badly with the time change Typos can do. Luckily he did not dwell on it. Our position in the circle is different, you'll see, and there's a chant which initially you'll think you will never learn.' I stopped and smiled at him. 'Over the years you will. There is always an old hand who leads, don't worry. I can't tell you their names, no one knows them, they are known only by the country name.

'I suppose I ought to say that just recently, as it's near Christmas, I have started bringing a seasonal bottle of fizz for them, but that had never been usual.'

I paused, letting it sink in a bit, waiting for questions. None came.

'They are a good bunch, and don't worry, this is our validation if you like, for the spring forces. By the way, the river, wind and all Typos demands I have never, ever discussed.'

He sat quietly, and out of the corner of my eye I could see his hands churning in his lap.

'We will be there in about half an hour I reckon, how you doing?'

'Yes, I am fine but…' he stopped.

'Go on, fire away, be brave.'

'Look, it's no big deal, but can I ask you a tiny personal thing?'

'Of course, I have no secrets.' I laughed and said back, dreading what he would ask. What was he going to fire at me? I had always been straight with him. Getting the concept of his new position across to him had been murder.

'Well all right, it's only a silly thing really, but others have said the same thing to me. They have noticed that you always have near you, well, within seeing distance, a bird, to be specific a buzzard. People have seen it and remarked, have you been a falconer or something? It is always in sight, I have got used to it.'

I unashamedly laughed aloud. 'Thank goodness, Will. Is that all? You had me seriously worried.'

Between giggling, which got Will going in sympathy too, I explained.

'My position, well yours too now, has been watched for generations. The buzzards have a duty, a watching brief. They are always discreet, never obvious, unless you look, but it is their time-honoured duty. Way way back, I was hacking my horse, well to be honest mucking about a bit, and anyway he fell. I found myself in hospital, my first time. A buzzard called Mewlic kept a record of all, and weird as it may seem he told my then hound, who told me. You see, when I am a goner, they will be there for you just the same! So there, it makes sense. They are not trained birds, just doing their job.'

In between wrestling with the gear stick, I turned my head briefly to him, catching his eye and smiling.

'That is incredible!' he said. 'There's a lot to you, isn't there? I will not tell a soul, don't worry. Amazing!' he muttered repeatedly.

Up the final rise before our turn and there on the left were the awesome stones, looking formidable in the now failing light.

'You think that is amazing? Wait until you see this. We are there now, look, there is Stonehenge. We use the car park on the other side, but actually we go behind the henge. Wait until it's virtually dark, and definitely no people. Some years we have had to wait a fair while.'

We pulled into the gravelled car park and looking around, I was pleased to see three cars I recognised. But we were not yet alone. A coachload of schoolgirls were loading up. They were all laughing and mucking about, clutching work books. Shepherding them together and then onto the coach were two weary-looking teachers, repeatedly counting their charges and looking around for missing ones.

'We'll sit and wait until they all go' I said.

The rain eased and the sun finally sank out of sight, leaving a red glow in the sky. Wiping the condensation from the windscreen, I looked across to see two cars' internal lights come on as doors opened. Very soon the third driver's door opened and with hands raised in greeting, they all started walking towards us.

'Here we go, come on' I said to Will, pulling my seat belt off and opening the door. 'See, I told you, the rain has stopped.'

Outside the three main watchers and two followers stood smiling a greeting.

'Remember, no names' I whispered under my breath to Will, pleased to see him nod back. We walked over, and standing in that car park in the failing light I went around introducing Will to them all. I knew of course that this was also my goodbye, the last time I would be there.

I have said in the past that it takes just a fraction of a second to assess someone as a friend and work out their character, and these chaps over the years have all been brilliant. All individuals, relaxed and completely at one with their timeless traditional duties, with no daft attitudes, just thinking of their responsibility. We all share the beautiful Beltane image and feel honoured to ensure its continuance.

'This man is Wales,' I pointed across for Will, and both stuck out their hands. A tall, elderly man wearing an old waxproof over moleskin trousers, he had a nut-brown face, with lumps of black hair sticking out from under an old and greasy flat cap. His voice when he spoke to Will later was musical, softly rising and falling, enchanting and very gentle.

He turned to introduce, again no names, his follower, a youngish lad who admittedly looked a little worried by everything. At this point I could feel that with the newness of it all he had a problem. Will had picked up on his tension and I was so pleased to see him spend a while with this newcomer as well.

Scotland had been new possibly twenty years before. He was a shorter, very relaxed man with a full beard. He too was buried in an old waxproof - obviously the sky had worried these chaps. A large polo neck showed at his neck, with old ripped jeans stuffed in equally ancient green Hunter wellies. He has always said very little; it seems a trait with these chaps from Scotland - and when he did speak it was almost a whisper. You had to concentrate, not wanting to appear rude. He always had such a ready smile though that you could not help but smile back.

Finally the Irish watcher, who had his own follower behind. These two seemed well bonded, with the elder now and then joshing and throwing the odd air punch. They were a good-humoured pair, although they had had the longest journey. To be honest, on reflection, once things got started the young Irish follower seemed most involved and I did see later that evening that his elder had his arm over his shoulders, whispering, I suppose, reassurance or explanation.

So that evening, my last was also the last for two other watchers; it's funny how things work out.

'We will begin, dark is nearly here, come on' Scotland said, turning and walking off into the gloom. We all followed, the two younger ones whispering 'hello' on the way across the shingle to the grass.

The atmosphere of the stone circle is all-embracing. The stones stood almost religiously, importantly, just tolerating our presence, it seemed, and watching us as they had done for centuries. The slight drizzle had stopped, and as we walked the car headlights from the nearby road disappeared as the ground rose between us and them.

We do not go fully into the stone circle, but join, holding hands. This time I was standing in the middle. I nodded to Will, as he looking worried and was staying on the circle edge. I motioned to him to join hands and just watch. The other two new followers mouthed 'all right' and smiled. They appeared happy enough at that moment.

To the outsider stumbling across us this could look pagan, some sort of black mass. It is nothing of the sort, for the events we see are real, nothing to do with religion. The events are to do with natural law, natural forces. They are beyond man's imagination and date back to before the dawn of history.

At a spoken signal from Wales we started our simple, repetitive chant. A half-moon began to rise in the sky, adding a little light. No wind lifted our hair and all the world seemed quiet, even the background noise of the cars had gone.

Out of habit, standing in the middle with arms outstretched to my side, I shut my eyes, joining with the ancient chant. The other main players rhythmically joined this refrain, and soon it seemed to fill the air. After a moment, with my eyes half open, I could see that our new watchers were standing wide-eyed and even apprehensive, each locked in hands with his neighbour.

Then, through the autumn dark, a tawny owl called, its screech splitting the night. Within a moment another two joined in, the first from a distance and the second nearby. Then came that moment, that magical moment, when I felt a slight wind on my face and one of the owls, without a sound, flew in and alighted on my arm. It landed on my jacket sleeve with no weight at all, its talons only just detectable through the fabric.

At that point the air became full of owl calls, a tremendous magical noise filling the air. From their calls there seemed to be tawny and barn owls galore, and I am no expert on bird calls but little owls I am sure arrived too. It is of course hard to be precise, but it sounded as if hundreds of owls had arrived to join in. The air was full of calls, enchanting and wonderful. I have always known their purpose and felt honoured to be involved, that night as always.

I looked along my arm at the tawny, which was intent on calling, pushing her chest out, head back, and looking about her. Every now and then she would bob down, perhaps in some signal or acknowledgement. Her head turned to me and looked deep into my eyes, clicking and grinding her beak. She bobbed to me, then took off to fly in front of me.

One common factor with so many birds around us and no wind is the smell of bird feather dander hanging in the air; a distinctive perfume, never forgotten.

And then suddenly the sky was empty and the night was silent;

the owls had gone. This has always been one of the saddest moments of the year. It is a magical moment which I always wanted to go on longer, at least longer than the ten minutes or so that it does.

I put my arms down and said nothing, but looked around the group. The old hands half smiled, lost in their thoughts perhaps, for as with me, this was their last. The new ones looked stunned, half smiling. It is the same with all new folk to this function, the history, and responsibility is brought home.

'How was that Will, what did you think?' I said, going over to him. He was speechless, shaking his head,

'That has brought it all home to me, it is so important. I mean... I've seen some weird stuff this last eighteen months, but that just reinforced how important this all is. I mean it has got nothing to do with, I don't know, chemical, nuclear, this is our world.' He stopped and looked up at me. 'This is heavy stuff, important, real...' he put his head down, shaking his head. 'Wonderful - wonderful!'

I smiled, remembering my first view of this with Jules.

'That was our verification, our authority' called out Wales, for the benefit of the newcomers, the new watchers.

'Yes you are so right' Scotland said, pulling his collar up. 'Come on, home time until next year, same day, some of you have got a long journey, go safely.'

We started walking back to the cars, and began to say our goodbyes. One after another the others drove away, leaving just Will and me.

'Let me tell you Will, after my ding with Shola it took Typos a while to find out where I should be' I said to him. 'She flew me here – well, over there' – I pointed through the dark - 'and it was so difficult, you would not believe it, to arrive without a car. Well, Typos was of course hidden. I had to pretend I had got a lift. Then of course one of the guys offered me a lift back. Nightmare.'

I smiled across at him. 'I hope that filled any gaps and made sense. It will be your thing when I am gone.'

I went silent for a moment, lost in my thoughts, thinking back to all the times I had been there before.

'If it helps at first, keep a diary to remind you. Write in a code, for goodness sake, just for you. The spring queen, the Wind Furies, this of course, and the river. You are chosen, but cannot miss any of them. They are all, without being dramatic, vital for all people... you have been chosen!'

'Well it may sound odd, but I am a little touched by this, humbled even. Why should I have this honour? It's unreal. I am lost!' He looked at his hands, seeming sad, even tearful.

'Come on, you are it, you have no choice, you're honoured. And you'll know you are unique all your life. Think of what you have seen and done so far. I hate them really, but they have a place. Right, come on, I feel the need for a burger on the way back, from the nearest roadside job.'

The engine caught and we drove out of the car park, onto the homeward road. Chatting about nothing in particular we began our drive back, and with the addition of a double burger with plastic cheese, humour returned to Will, or at least he lost some of his seriousness. But as we buzzed back, radio blaring, one of those moments arrived which make you wonder why.

The radio was playing old hits and the reception was fair to abysmal, the hills muting it badly. Through the hiss and fizz an old tune by the most famous Swedish band could just be heard. I started humming and then, as I drove, singing. Will joined in, whether to humour me or not I was not sure.

'They were a couple of lookers, weren't they?' he asked, turning to me.

'They were, but they were my generation, not yours.'

'Ah! seen so many old videos, great old tunes, proper tunes, and a pair of ravers, all my mates still think so.'

I laughed. 'Timeless. All blokes are the same.'

'Well it is true all Swedes have those looks, you only have to go back to Freyja to learn that.'

To say I nearly crashed with this remark would not be far off the mark. I swerved across the road, but luckily nothing was coming.

'Watch out! You OK?' shouted Will across at me.

I had the presence of mind to calm down and change the subject. 'See that deer by the side of the road? Well, I wonder I didn't hit it.'

'No, I didn't see a deer' said Will, screwing his head around to look out of the back window. 'No sign of it back there anyway.'

Peace returned, but inwardly I was in turmoil. Then after a while another reasonable tune started playing, and I drummed my fingers on the wheel, hoping to appear nonchalant. Trying to sound as casual as possible, I asked 'What were you saying, and who was she – Freyja, did you say?'

He began an account which stunned me and threw me into turmoil. At college they had been studying as a course extra the old gods and deities that had ruled lives in the past, and in fact only last term had been going over Norse mythology. The teacher had used several examples of Swedish and Norwegian beauties to get over to his late adolescent pupils that one Freyja had been famous for her beauty.

'She was a looker then?' I asked casually, concentrating like mad on driving while not wanting to appear too interested. He went on to say that they had spent a whole week on her. She was stunningly attractive and equal in power to Thor, a fertility goddess of great love and beauty. She led the Valkyrie, taking the souls of wounded warriors to feast with her in Odin's hall. They had winged horses. She was considered, he added, a source of good deeds in the world, a healer, and responsible for all things to do with love and peace.

Then the remark that did for me came. 'Oh yes, she had tame cats as friends, and a boar.'

Like an idiot, without thinking, I muttered 'Hildisvini!'

'That's right, you do know!' shouted Will. 'Well remembered.'

'It was just a name that stuck with me, not sure why' I lied.

Then the final remark, nonchalantly said by Will as he reached for a pineapple chunk. 'Oh yes, she has a really neat cloak made of feathers, that she used to lend to people to fly' He paused a moment. 'And there's another thing, she had a necklace made by dwarves but she had to sleep with all of them to get it. Payment if you like, lucky dwarves!'

I was too stunned to say anything, and just nodded in agreement. 'Sounds amazing' was all I said.

The rest of the journey I do not really remember, but I do recall that Will could not stay for a cuppa that night. In the yard, crash helmeted, engine running, he waved goodbye. I smiled at him. 'Be safe Will, see you soon'.

In a cloud of exhaust he left, and I went in to see the dogs, and to think.

CHAPTER 11

A VISIT DURING IMBOLC

I awoke the next morning with a massive headache; I remember it to this day. It was almost certainly caused by not sleeping at all well that night. I tossed and turned as all that Will had told me seemed perpetually to be going through my head.

Finally, as a weak sun peeped through the morning clouds, I gave in, got dressed and wandered down to the pile of dogs in the kitchen. Surprised to see me so early, they stretched, opened their eyes and rolled upside down for tummy tickling.

'Hello you lot, let me open the door' I said. I put the kettle on and reached for the aspirin. Those and some toast and two mugs of tea went a long way towards making me feel better, and having fed the dogs and left them for a moment I went to consult my encyclopaedias. I have to admit that I did not often consult them, and that morning it took me a while to find them all. I also had to shift a fair amount of dust from their spines.

After a few moments' research I sat back, horrified and stunned by what I had found. I had no problem with confirming what I felt

I knew about my Freyja, but I felt weak when I found out how much did not know. I remember that in fact my hands shook a little and I began to feel slightly sick with all I had read. I could just get my head around the fact that she was recorded as a goddess from history, was the daughter of Niord and had lived in her hall, Sessrumnir in Asgard, the realm of the gods. I confirmed with a touch of jealousy that she had won her Brisingamen necklace by sleeping with the dwarves who had made it. She had led the Valkyrie, who on winged horses had collected the souls of the slain warriors, taking them back to her father's halls for reward. History had her linked to fertility, beauty, love, war and death. I also confirmed that she had been stunningly beautiful.

But then I sat holding my head in hands as I learned that she had a husband and two daughters, Hnoss and Gersemi. I had tried to question her gently on her life, relationships and so on, and realised that on this she had told me little. It all drove me slightly mad with doubt and concern. How could I have met someone from history?

Freyja's husband had apparently been a god, Oor, who went missing, and then I read that she often searched for him, crying tears of real gold. Her name had appeared in many poems, songs and Scandinavian folklore.

As I read this again and again I thought back to my first meeting with this woman by the woodland pool, how she had resisted my questions and cried tears that ran like gold at her feet.

As I learnt some more, the fact that she had cats and a boar companion became incidental to the fact that somehow, with Typos' help, I had met this figure from ancient history figure in reality; and to add to my thoughts, that morning she had hinted at my joining her on my death.

To add insult to injury, and my mental turmoil that morning, I could not call her and I could not contact her, though I desperately wanted to.

I wandered back into the kitchen, thinking that a quick slug of instant coffee was the answer. This made and heavily sugared, I turned to calling the dogs. Clutching my mug, I went into the garden to think.

It was one of those damp, drizzly mornings, the sun barely visible. The hillsides were lost in the damp mist and hardly showed through the thick air. A pheasant called, making India jerk up excitedly. I laughed and said 'no not now', then carried on my aimless wandering down to the orchard, turning things over in my head. It had been drummed into me that I could not call Typos for just a minor thing, but for me this was vital, and after all I rationalised I would be dead, or rather different in less than a year, so what the hell? On reflection I cannot have been not a great companion for the dogs that morning, but they never challenged me or interfered.

I locked the doors, had a brief natter to my old hunter and walked up the hill. I can admit to you that I often stopped, wondering if what I was doing was right or would cause a problem, but I was being driven by my torment.

The grass in front of the barn was soaking wet, laden with droplets of water. The air up here on the hill was still, the view heavily restricted now by a low cloud layer. It was one of those mornings when as a child you would shout at the mist and hear your muted echo.

No birds were singing and all was sleepy in the hedges, but as I quietly walked across, lost in my thoughts, a red-brown dog fox got up from the hedge bottom in front of me. He turned to look for just a second then took off, running flat out down the field edge, heading down the hill. I watched him disappear in the mist, just catching the musty smell he left behind.

In front of the barn, it took a lot of resolve to begin the call. Wandering up and down, I dejectedly kicked out at the odd thistle heads, getting crosser with myself by the minute.

In the end my resolve hardened, and grabbing the stanchion for support I lowered myself down, out of habit closing my eyes after making a final check that I really was alone.

The chant began, softly and still hesitantly, but soon my bravery increased and began accelerating, almost on its own. Filling my head and every pore of my body, it took over, claiming me.

I almost expected my head to burst when I knew she had arrived. The lemony leather tang in the air was almost overpowering, and the feeling of being in the presence of a large power was awesome. It has always felt like this; the world seems to stop, With my eyes still firmly shut, the ripping of her talons in the turf filled my head.

As always, on opening my eyes I experienced immediate contact, an invasion of my thoughts, a full mental joining. Typos looked her usual immense, powerful self. Her greenish-yellow scales glistened with a moist sheen and the muscles rippled visibly under her skin. One of her talons was broken off, small pieces of meat remains jammed between her front leg talons, old blood evident. Her great tail worked slowly from side to side, making great swishing noises as it flattened grass and dead nettle stalks.

She opened her wings and lifted them up, stretching, then brought them almost so far forward that they looked over her head.

With a rustling noise they were settled back into her sides, and she turned her head back down to me.

Her head almost on my level, her breath filled my senses, a nauseating, dead meat, an abattoir smell.

'Myrrdin, you have need' she thought to me, shifting her weight.

'Well... not exactly... well yes,' I stammered back. I know I cannot call you for personal - er - matters. But I have no other option. I am lost.'

I stopped momentarily as her posture changed, becoming more erect for a moment. Then she looked me straight in the eye.

'You are not telling all, I know.' I was aware of her probing my thoughts.

'Freyja is filling your thoughts. Tell me now' she almost commanded.

' Well... how can it be that she does not seem old? She should be wrinkled, at least. It is not right, it seems wrong. I have got my head around the fact that you can go back in your time - well a little anyway. We have stories, accounts of her from years and years ago,. so how can it be that now she seems younger than me?'

'You like her' she replied sharply, seeing the truth.

It would be an understatement to deny that this rather hit the spot. I fiddled about in my head trying to get a straightforward answer, once again simply forgetting that with Typos, this was as good as talking to her.

'In your history is your union with her. It will happen soon, as I promised.'

'But that cannot happen! Can it? Does it?'

I fell silent, lost in a hopeless mix of thoughts.

'Get on now!' ordered Typos. 'I will show you things to help it make sense to you.'

'What, right now? You cannot show me anything, surely?'

'Yes do it, we go.' She said this with a tone I had met before. I knew that argument was unwise. Without saying anything else, I went around to her side, putting my hand on her scaly neck. She bent her head down, stretching her wings for balance, neck extended. With my usual wriggling and clumsy manoeuvring, I settled down between the spines on her neck, my legs wrapped around her neck just in front of her great leathery wings.

'I am fine' I thought to her.

'I go, you look, back just to what you call Mabon, your last month worship. Then we go back again.'

I was about to say 'what?' when she leapt into the air, turning as she jumped. The force pushed my teeth together, and it was obvious to me from the launch that she was a little annoyed.

'Look Typos, I'm sorry, I'm confused. I need your help.' I paused, then gave her neck a friendly squeeze with my legs, concerned that somehow I had offended her, or annoyed her. I felt that somehow I was in the wrong and I was mortified.

She climbed up, her wings beating hard, through a wispy cloud layer.

'I should not be here' she thought back, dare I say rather curtly. Then, before I could imagine how to reply, she said, 'It is fine, you are my first Myrrdin, I allow and will now help, I know your problem.'

I began to relax a little and began to feel marginally happier.

'Where do we go, what have you done, when is this?'

I had realised that in her initial great jump she had twitched back. We had gained a great height and it was much colder, but looking down I could see that she had worked east, and below us the countryside still looked autumnal. Strangely, all the major roads had gone, and the wooded areas seemed much bigger than before and the fields much smaller. Down below us a great tree trunk being pulled by three shire horses came into view, just leaving the edge of a great wooded area.

'This is the turn of the last century for you, before the great stupidity of wars began' she very matter-of-factly thought back. 'I will show you something older and later when we go back again. You just need to look, all will be plain in time. I cannot go back any further, it will be my limit.'

As she glided on I tried to skew my head around to look down at the horses. They were being led by an old man, who was nearly bent double. A young boy jumped around behind the horses, waving a small stick to encourage them on and dancing to and fro. The stump they were dragging had obviously just been cut; it still had green ivy wrapping its trunk. All three people were wearing what from our height looked like baggy canvas clothing, with the elderly fellow also wearing the pelt of some animal as a jacket. By modern standards they looked poor and the boy seemed cold and pinched, despite his activity.

Typos loitered as the light began to fail. Below us a stack of rooks made their noisy way to roost. Looking further into the fading red sky I could see small fires started, three then four, growing bigger as wood was thrown on. Their smoke rose into the now windless dusk night.

'Your day length is the same as the night today, this is important,' she said.

'I know' I thought back, 'this is the autumn equinox, in September, is that right?'

'Yes. To honour the forest god, you will see him tonight. They cannot, it is better. He is called Mabon.'

I was momentarily stunned by being told this. 'I have been seeing the spring being woken for many years now...'

Typos quickly butted in.

'Enough, do not tell. That is for you, not for me'.

'I am sorry.'

It was now dark, with a moon beginning to appear and just a hint of stars. We began to circle above over one of the bigger fires.

'We will go down to watch, do not...'

'I know, get off!' I joked back, giving her neck a big squeeze as she flared out on a patch of rough grass, on a slight rise above the fire. By the light of the fire below us, a column of people could just be made out approaching a crude wooden altar. The smoke twirled around. giving out the smell of wood burning, not at all unpleasant.

This was just a simple wooden table with odd knobbly legs, already laden with what looked like bottles of wine, big flagons of a liquid that might have been cider or mead and great platters of dried fruits and nuts. The whole dale was further adorned with great bunches of tied-up herbs.

More people began entering the dale, most of them carrying something, either herbs, flagons, fruit or what looked to be bunches of larger prickly herbs. All spoke gently to each other, a feeling of intense calm filling the air. There was no chanting, praying or anything like that, but as the night began they fell into a hush, the only noise being the crackle of the burning wood. Now and then one of the men threw another great brand on the fire. They all looked reflective, lost in meditation, as if going over what they had achieved.

A few of the children had been picked up, and I could see at least two swaddled babies fast asleep lulled in their mothers' arms.

'He is here. He comes' from Typos.

I was just about to say 'where?' when on the other side of the fire, lit by the blaze, there appeared an elderly man. He was carrying a long staff, and leaning on it as he looked around smiling. In the light from the fire, his baggy green clothes seemed to hang on him. He was thin to say the least, a bag of bones it seemed. He was hatless, with a big flowing crop of white hair spilling down into a long, long beard.

He stood turning his head around, smiling and taking note of it all. The people seemed unaware of him. His head slowly turned our way, and on looking towards us, he smiled. It was a massive grin that split his face. He lifted his staff with one hand and with the other he waved at Typos.

'Oh no, he has seen you!' I thought to her.

'It is not unusual, many times, we know each other. You people have called him the Green Man, but also Persephone and Modron.'

I lifted a hand in a rather feeble acknowledgement, feeling more than a tad out of my depth.

'He goes soon, is done.'

As she said this the Green Man turned, giving a last wave to us. He looked over his shoulder and left the clearing and the firelight. All the time the people in front had been quietly standing in front of the fire, completely unaware that they had been seen.

'Now we go back to your time, your year, but further to the falling sun.'

'Fine' was all I could inadequately think back.

The sky paled again, and I must admit to having a slight sensation of nausea as she twitched. Below us the motorway lights appeared, a seemingly endless stream of lights coming towards us, and red brake lights on the other side.

'This is quieter and less common, harder to find now' thought Typos to me. 'Your people ignore the old original forces, but they are wrong!'

At the time I did not really appreciate what she was meaning, but later, of course, I realised that paganism, if you want to call it that, is out of favour now.

After maybe twenty minutes of gentle flying into a light wind, with the land below now black as we had turned away from roads, in a valley bottom a growing fire could be seen. In the dark around it, a handful of dim figures moved about.

'We go down again to watch, if you get off, you are your time, but they can see.'

'Don't worry, I shall stay here, no fear.' I gave her neck a big pat. I have to say that I am not even sure she registers this at all, but she probably does hear my hand falling against her.

Typos flared down onto a paddock edge and ponderously walked back, so that we could look down over a fence then down into the ghyll. As before, wooden tables were set up on the fire edge, and they already carried great bowls.

From the boots of two parked cars, an endless stream of sacks were being carried to the table. Some conversation was carried to us, mention of grains, vegetables, pine cones, sage, and then, surprisingly, one lady mentioned that she had the 'thistles'.

With everything apparently in place they all went over to a

barn on the side. When they reappeared they were suited and dressed up and appeared quite elegant.

The two women were not over made-up but looked very smart. They were wearing brooches, and one wore a necklace glinting in the fire light.

The night darkened and the group stood in the firelight, with little conversation coming to us. They were all drinking from glasses of wine.

'Here he is' thought Typos, shifting her feet.

'What, the Green Man again?' I thought back in complete disbelief. In the flickering light on the far side I saw him. He looked exactly the same. 'This is later, a different time. I felt you twitch, felt sick. How can he be the same?'

'I have told you before, your time concept is wrong. Why I bring you here now.'

As she thought this to me, the Green Man had turned his head to us. He looked momentarily stunned and took a step back. Then he broke into his now easily recognisable smile. Flinging his staff down, he lifted both hands to us in a greeting.

Typos nearly threw me off as she bowed down, dropping her head to the ground.

As I wriggled back up, I looked and felt his eyes on me. Looking across, I smiled, and was delighted to see him smile back, lifting one hand in greeting.

'He has seen, will go now!'

Almost at her order it seemed, he turned and left. As before, the group of people seemed completely unaware of him.

'We stay and watch' thought Typos to me, walking back along the fence line, her gait rolling, which made it harder for me to keep my balance. The group below us split up, all carrying bottles and flagons to the trees on the forest edge. When they got to them they began pouring wine and cider on the tree roots, uttering a form of words of some kind as they did so.

I wanted to know why and what it all meant. I was stunned to know that through all the years this was being carried out by so few. All my life I had had no inkling, and after all, my life had been unusual, to say the least, so far.

'This goes from children to children, years upon years, starting before me, with my mother,' came from Typos. I could not answer, lost in the immensity of what she had shown me, the timeless rituals happening for each generation. I have to admit to being thoroughly confused as to how the Green Man had appeared years later unchanged, and no older.

'I will show you one more to help you. We go now.' Before I could answer, she bounded skywards, turning back to the east. As she rose a massive twitching happened and this time I did throw up. It left me feeling rough and with a vile taste in my mouth. Obviously the movement had registered.

'You are fine?'

'Yes, fine' I muttered, feeling ready to vomit again.

'Good. We now go further back, nearly to my start, I don't know what you say – when your people were simpler.'

With this she thought no more. Peering below me into the dusky half-light, all the countryside was black and indiscernible. A silvery river then showed up and following along in the near black, I could just make out where it met the sea. The waves showed up as luminescence, the river now wider. Soon tiny flakes of snow filled the air, telling me that she was flying higher, to get over the cloud. It became get bitingly cold and I pushed my hands under me, next to her skin. This she must have felt, despite her wing muscles contracting firmly,

'It is not long, we are back to nearly when I started. You say I think seventeen.'

'What, the seventeenth century?'

'Yes my start, as far back as I can go, we will see below us. Your people called 'Imbolc', nearly one of your four main times.'

Frankly I was too perplexed to ask anything. I just sat there, watching the rare light below us and getting colder and colder.

'Your sheep are now full.'

'What, with lambs?' I thought back, thinking we must be in about February, remembering the old farming calendar. A few farmers still lamb early like this to catch a market, but I have always aimed to lamb onto the new grass much later.

'We will watch one of your water heads, a well, you say. This is old, and we will see it has been changed.' I must admit that at this point she had completely lost me.

After perhaps another twenty minutes or so, she began to go down through the sleet. It became thicker in patches, with big flakes that began to stick to us. I spent a while brushing them off, poking my tongue out to taste the odd one that settled on my hand or face.

Below us a narrow track through fields came into view, the fields either side carrying a white skin of snow. The lane petered out into a track which was well marked with footprints, the mud underneath showing through. The track stopped at a stone-walled and thatched building, and in the fields to one side Typos put in. The snow crunched audibly under her feet.

'Aren't we a bit close, Typos?' I whispered to her.

'I cannot move, they will see my prints in this white.'

'Oh! of course I understand.' I had forgotten that although fractionally behind real time, which is why they are not seen, footprints can be seen after they are made.

At this moment, with her just settled, a small group of well-wrapped-up people came along the track. Two carried buckets and led the way into the building, re-emerging with splashing, filled buckets. What talk that came on the air to us was general chat, very hard to understand, like a foreign tongue. It then became noticeably more serious as the rest of the group of women and children came forward to the front. Two of the children appeared to be carrying cross shapes woven out of rushes. The adults carrying food on platters, blankets and flasks of what I took to be wine.

'This is all for her goddess, Brighid,' one muttered.

The two elderly ladies going into the building were obviously making a bed out of the blankets, and presumably arranging the plates of food and the drink flasks.

The whole group reformed at the front, and then after a little good-natured back-slapping, face-kissing, hugs and a final look around, they started walking off.

'We will wait, she will come, we wait' thought Typos to me.

'Fine' was all I could return. I have to admit that I was starting to get very cold and wondering what would happen, but then I heard footsteps from the well side and a bent, fully-cloaked figure appeared. Shuffling along, seemingly with little energy, she was stopping at nearly every stride. Wisps of blonde, almost white hair escaped from the shawl covering her head, and now and then puffs of exhaled air hung in front of her.

As we stayed watching this figure, she stopped, slowly turning her head up and towards us and I saw a beautiful elderly lady with piercing brown eyes gazing at us. Before I could think a warning to Typos, the lady smiled and mouthed 'welcome' to us. Her smile was infectious.

Typos, and this will sound bizarre, bowed slightly to her. Once again I nearly took a purler at this. Fighting to get snug back between her neck spines, I turned to look again back at the lady and was surprised to see her clutching her sides in joyful laughter.

She now looked about thirty years younger, and I admit to starting to laugh back. She lifted her hands to say goodbye, smiled, and went into the well.

'This is old Imbolc, with Brighid, we now go back to your time. We go.' Her usual bound had us airborne, and as I tried to look down over her shoulders, I felt her twitch. This time, possibly as I had puked already, nothing happened, just the vile noise. I settled down, glad to feel some warmth coming from Typos' body.

She seemed to be flying with a vengeance, very low and fast. Below us, many lit-up houses appeared and reassuringly a road went below us, with many feeder roads joining and leaving it. After a few moments a pair of headlights came and went below us, and in the distance the many lights and buildings of a largish sea port appeared.

I have always relished flying at speed, with hedges and building whipping underneath. I was cold, hungry and stiff, but it was unreal, and when Typos went even lower and we crossed the sea, I nearly whooped with joy.

'Where on earth are you going, you loon?' I thought to her.

'This is your Manx.'

'You mean the Isle of Man.'

'Yes, I suppose, near your time, but before your birth.'

I could think no more at that point and looked down as the island appeared. She did not fly very far inland, alighting as dusk arrived by the side of a village lane along which four houses stood.

'We wait and keep still and quiet' thought Typos. As we waited and watched, women appeared at their doors, throwing rushes on the ground in some cases, or laying a blanket across the door hearth. They appeared to be reciting something at the air, and I heard one say 'The door is open for you Brede, come in, be welcome'.

Two women disappeared into an open barn on the other side of the lane. They had gone in with platters of food and blankets, to come out with empty hands. Through the barn doors as the dark fell, the candles they had left behind began to throw a flickering yellow light. The local blackbirds stopped pinking at each other, two dogs on the village edge stopped barking and the night closed in.

I could hardly believe it when the same shuffling elderly figure appeared around the barn edge. Typos moved as if to catch her attention, and she raised her head and looked across. I knew it was the same woman, but she looked somehow younger, her body posture less bent. She still walked slowly, but looked firmer and more determined. She stopped to look at us with a smile. It was a wondrous smile, full of humour and affection. Lifting both hands in welcome, I waved back with a big grin on my face.

Typos shuffled on one foot then the other as we watched her walk on from house to house before going into the barn, leaving us both happy, me grinning like a loon.

'Your people now call her Saint Brighid, do you say church... took over her?' thought Typos to me. 'We go back to yours now.'

With a gentle jump this time and even more gentle twitching she began powering back. Now I have resisted thinking to her whilst airborne, as it did not feel right to intrude, but this time I was bursting to ask her all sort of things.

'When we return we will talk and get your fears and plan for you. This is right now. When we finish.'

She must have read my mind.

CHAPTER 12

A MISSION IN THE MOUNTAINS AND MY FUTURE

I hoped that over the next few days Typos would call me, but she did not. There is no point on me dwelling on the mental purgatory I went through over the next few weeks, but you can imagine, I'm sure.

Thinking back now, it was probably only a few weeks later that Will and I were called. The spring warmth had arrived with a vengeance. In shirt sleeves I bent and crawled my slow way across vegetable patches, and the grass was leaping out of the ground; the hay crop promised well. Fruit buds were expanding on the trees and the flower patches were dazzling. I pootled about, talking to the dogs and taking the occasional slow wander with my old hunter.

I was perpetually thinking of Freyja and longing to call her. I suppose I was not willing to call Typos again, despite being desperate for contact with her too. I knew that last time it had been barely tolerated. She had left me that last night thinking to me that on our next meeting she would go over a plan for my future.

I had just wandered in for my usual afternoon cuppa, and was rooting through tins looking for a bit of cake. The dogs had arrived, hearing the tins, and all sat expectantly in a circle on the kitchen flags. I have to admit to chucking them a bit each on these occasions. Why not? We are all old, yet we stay slim.

As I fished the teabag out of my cup with a teaspoon, the call began. I remember the urgency in it. I was momentarily stunned to hear the tinny noise of Will's scooter arrive in the yard at almost the same time. Looking through the open kitchen door, I had just lifted a hand in greeting when I saw him bend double and clutch at his head. My call was going, and I knew what he was feeling. The dogs stopped in their tracks, tails wagging.

Bumble lifted his head and turned to me. 'Are you called?' he thought, obviously worried by Will's posture.

'Don't worry old chum, mine is over. Yes, we are needed. His call will pass.'

Will raised his head, managing a faint smile, as he pulled his skidlid off.

'Ah. I hate that, at least I didn't puke that time.'

He wiped at his mouth, then bent down to ruffle and pat the pack of welcoming dogs.

'The timing is weird, I was only coming over to see you have a natter and nick one of your cakes.' He looked up and smiled at me.

'Later I am afraid, my lad' I replied, smiling back. 'When we are back. Hang on there will you? I'll lock up. Can you settle the dogs in? We'll go up the hill and hear what we have to witness.'

I reached down a couple of old jackets hanging on the back of the door.

'Here bung that on, although it is warmish now, you never know with Typos. Could be the Arctic we are going next' I joked.

We walked up the lane, me going as fast as I could, Will politely slowing his normal gambol. We both climbed over the gate. Oddly, it had become easier to do than wrestling with the ancient padlock and chain.

A light wind came at us on the hill top, and although the sun peeped through light clouds there was a chill to the air, despite the summer on the horizon.

We wandered over to the barn, taking a quick glance at the ewes. They stopped grazing, a few expectantly calling to me, used to winter feed arriving. Several of them were getting large now, feeling new lambs move inside them, and soon my nights would be sleepless as lambing began. They would be started on a protein ration next week in anticipation of lambing, and brought in at night. It was easier to check them over when they were in and it helped to keep unexpected early lambs safe from foxes and stray dogs.

'They all look all right, come on, let's move on. Do you want to call her today?'

I asked looking across at Will.

'Right, yes… yes I will. You will be there?'

'Of course!' I laughed back. 'By the way, have you thought where you are going to call her, when it is just you?'

'Well there is an old barn in a field behind us, it's not used and the owner is a nice old boy. He has known me since I was tiny and doesn't mind me wandering about. Dad mentioned to him that if he ever wants to sell the paddock it's in, to let him know. You never know, it might be Dad's one day.'

He stopped and turned to me, putting a hand out to hold my arm for a moment, a sad look on his face.

'But it's not going to be years yet, is it?'

'Well, you never know' I answered, looking him straight in the eye and smiling. 'You can never be sure. I'm not going to last forever, and you are my replacement you know. Look, I can tell you that when I peg it.' His face showed his fear. 'Not yet, don't worry' I quickly added. 'But when I do, well, all of this will be yours, provided you keep the dogs in a style they are accustomed to, and the old horse. The house will be your asset, you can rent it out or live in it. Up to you.'

'Stop saying that sort of stuff, I don't deserve it anyway. It's years off yet, eh?'

He stopped walking, turning to look at me for a moment, then shifted his stare to his feet. It was painfully obvious that he was embarrassed. 'I don't deserve all this, how could I. Crikey! We are not really even related... Just by our shared job, I suppose!'

'You never know Will, never know' I repeated.

As we walked on, though I could not tell him, all was planned, and I was utterly convinced that he was more than up to keeping this tradition going.

'Anyway, not now, we will talk about this later. Got to have plans' I said.

At the barn I was still rather lost in thought, and I absent-mindedly pulled at a creeper growing up the edge.

'Right, I'm set', called out Will. He was kneeling, his head turned up to me.

'Sorry, I was miles away.' I smiled and knelt down next to him, taking his offered hand to ease myself down. We both shut our eyes and he began to call her out loud, without any prompting and flawlessly. It seemed that almost immediately she was there, her talons ripping into the turf, the lemony smell very intense.

As an aside, and this may seem crude, but I have learnt over many years that this smell is stronger the more excited or shall I say wound up, that she is.

I smiled at this marvellous creature as she shimmered in the sun, flexing her muscles and stretching first one leg out to the side, then the other. With legs stretched, both wings were noiselessly extended, momentarily flapped and with a lot of shaking over her back, finally settled alongside her. She then turned those soft languid pools of eyes on to me, their blackness intense, and as I have told you before, she smiled.

I turned to look at a smiling Will, his eyes brimming with tears. 'Hey, don't be daft, you did it brilliantly, just brilliantly, Typos is here.'

'No not that, it is just that she… this is marvellous, incredible. She is beginning to get to me' he whispered.

We both struggled to our feet to go across to Typos and give her massive rough and scaly neck our usual greeting. This I know she likes.

'You are here, I am called. Now on, we must go, we are needed now.' She had a commanding tone. She lay down in front of the barn and Will and I climbed up on to her neck. Within two steps she was airborne and within a moment she had twitched. This time the time shift must have been small, as all around and now under us appeared unchanged.

As Will and I started looking at the familiar countryside below, Typos began clawing, with her muscular efforts obvious below us. She was heading straight for the sea, Chesil Beach coming into view as we approached. The tide was just on the turn and starting to come back in. A few people walked along the water's edge, and two dogs were swimming. In that light the water looked strikingly blue, with a few lazy rollers marching to the shore. They broke on the shingle edge and from our increasing height we could look along the beach towards Portland where it merges with the cliffs.

At perhaps six thousand feet, Typos' wings locked out straight. Then she began falling forward, the increasing wind making our eyes water and the muscles in our faces shake and vibrate. Through the wind I heard Will almost shouting in excitement. Typos had done this with me before, but it is always just as wonderful, and the obvious power she has is extraordinary.

When we had almost reached the sea and could begin to taste the spray, she began working her way up again, always in a straight line, giving us a good look at a ferry crossing below us. Within a very short time the coastline of France came into view.

'Typos, where are you needed? What are we about?' I thought to her, and heard Will grunt in agreement.

'Tugarin needs my help' she thought back.

To say that I was stunned at that name would be an understatement.

'Who - your friend from Russia? The one who came to help you avenge your mother's death, years ago?' My mind recalled that night with horror.

'Correct. She need us to watch a happening, and others are already busy, so we must help.'

I leaned forward, shaking Will by the shoulder, until he turned his head to me, his eyes questioning.

'Look Will, this is strange. I do not know yet what we will be seeing, but Typos is answering a call from a friend, Tugarin. You need to know that Tugarin is a bit different.' I paused. 'Well, a lot different actually.'

'What do you mean? What are you trying to say?'

I thought for a moment, then decided it was best that Will should be prepared for the apparition he would soon see.

'Well…' I paused, looking him straight in the eye. 'You have seen so much so far, got your head around demons, ghouls and dragons.'

'I cannot bear the thought of any more of those ghouls!' Will shouted back, turning his body to look at me straight.

'Hey don't worry, she is on our side' I smiled back, trying to be reassuring. 'She is Typos' friend, you have seen some of her others, remember?'

He nodded, still looking petrified.

'Well, Tugarin is a bit different, she is from Russia, and she has really large, paper-thin wings. In fact she cannot fly in rain at all, so she has to avoid it.'

As I reached this point Typos hit a massive air pocket, and dropped for perhaps thirty seconds like a brick. The air was noticeably cold and we could feel it falling with us as the ground sharpened up below. With a massive effort Typos fought her way out of it.

'This air has holes' was her only thought as she fought her way back up, rather nonchalantly I felt.

'Anyway I was saying,' I continued, 'She is a bit different - hard to look at.'

'What do you mean, what are you getting at? Tell me, for goodness sake!'

'Well, she has extra… she has three heads.'

'You're having me on!' he said, goggle eyed.

'No, it's true, you will see. I found it essential not to look too closely. I have to tell you that she is probably the weirdest thing you will ever see. Each head is separate and they'll will look at you intently. But remember, Typos is our mate, she'll protect us, she's on our side. So we are safe, there's no threat.'

I desperately wanted to lighten his thoughts and looking ahead, I saw the white peaks of the Alps. 'Hey look ahead, so glad we bunged our jackets on, look at the snow.'

'My geography is rubbish, but could that be Mont Blanc over there?' said Will. 'We have come many miles. It's unreal. We've covered so much ground.'

At this point Typos began thinking to us. 'There has been a fall of the white stuff you call snow.'

Before I could think back, a massive volume of dragonspeak filled our heads. So much so that Will rather pointlessly put his hands over both ears. Mercifully, we were soon aware of Typos' answering thoughts.

'Tugarin is there on the side, watching from above. He wants us to protect lower slopes. The humans begin to look, we will see soon.'

Her flying took us up a snow-laden slope and then through a gap between two smaller peaks. It was frankly breathtaking to look down on the valley slopes below. The upper snow was achingly white in the sun. Turning to look to the left, it was not difficult to imagine how a great mass of snow and ice had slide down. The top slopes had an almost translucent look, but lower down the slope, for possibly several thousand feet, the snow was rippled, heaped and ridged. It looked unstable, to say the least.

In the valley bottoms, the snow must have melted months before. Everything was green, the roads jet black in contrast, and here and there the odd tree in blossom could be seen.

Typos glided down to a snowy ridge half way down and with a massive snow flurry she landed. The ridge cracked under her weight, sending ice and compacted lumps of snow airborne below us. Her wings opened immediately, poised for taking off again.

'We wait... it is safe, we stay' she thought to us both, bringing her wings halfway in, as if waiting and testing her position.

'Look' pointed Will, straining to look over Typos head. 'They must be looking for survivors - walkers or climbers, I suppose.'

'Typos, where are we exactly, do you know?' I asked her. She did not answer straight away, and I realised she was communicating with Tugarin.

'Below us what you call chamois. Lots of humans are buried and now there are threats. It will pass soon.'

'There must have been an avalanche' I said to Will, pointing down the slope below us. 'Look!'

Below us a line of searchers, tiny dots, were crossing the slope, making very slow progress. At the ends of the line we could just make out heavy dogs, possibly German Shepherds, working to and fro in front. They were hundreds of feet below us, but slowly they were working up, heading across the slope, and frequently stopping, perhaps to listen, probing the snow with long rods and reforming so they kept straight.

Will had turned his head to look up at the topmost crest and I felt him tighten his grip in a panic and then start mumbling and pointing up the slope. I followed the direction he was pointing to see on the crest, standing out from the snow, and blue sky behind her, the massive shape of Tugarin. Having seen her once before I was half prepared for her size, but I have no problem admitting that my pulse quickened and I felt my bowels twitch at this truly horrid and frightening vision. This three-headed monster was sitting on the top ridge, with two of the heads on thin necks peering down into the valley. To my dismay, the last head was fixed on us.

'Don't worry, Typos will look after us' I whispered to Will, giving his shoulders a squeeze.

Each head had a red hackled crest which was standing out in the cold air. The long necks seemed to ripple, whilst the heads remained fixed, locked in position. Her body was a blackish grey and her wings were enormous, so large that they seemed to fold in and hang by her flanks. Now and then she opened them to regain her balance. Her legs seemed massive, though her talons were hidden by the snow.

All three heads turned at once to us, and we could feel their penetrating stare. Both Will and I turned away in fear to see right away below us the reason her gaze had changed.

Unseen by the line of advancing men, in the valley bottom below a hideous gangrel creature had begun climbing up the valley edge. As it made its slow progress it left in the air great trails of snow, mud and wet material. Even from this distance we could see that it was throwing its hideous head from side to side, seeming to scent the air. Its blood-red eyes peered through the snow as if its vision was poor. Now and then it threw its head up, licked its lips and opened its great mouth to show yellow fangs and utter a vile noise. It was blatantly questing for dead men, and I guessed that their souls were its prey.

To our dismay, rising snow plumes on the far side showed that it had a mate, which was working in from the other side of the valley.

Then the scene rapidly changed as without warning, up on the mountainside, Tugarin let out the most appalling roar. It seemed to fill the air, rocketing around the valley and causing another small avalanche to begin on the far side.

The line of men down below us stopped walking, looking across the valley at the falling snow and rapidly joining together. The ghoulish creatures had stopped in their tracks, and their hideous gaze had turned up to the dragon. She opened her wings to their full extent, and her three heads looked down the valley. The necks extended, flat and in line with the downhill terrain. From each head a piercing roar issued, producing a smaller snowfall on the far side, and then we saw the most extraordinary sight. From Tugarin's drawn-back lips and open mouths, great fiery blasts roared out.

The vile creatures below stopped momentarily, then reared up and let out hideous yells, shaking their front claws in the air. I realised the dragons were communicating.

Suddenly Typos reared up, opening her wings. Whilst Will and I struggled back into some sort of position, a massive fiery blast came from her. Frighteningly hot and smelling of fireworks, it lit up the side of the valley where we sat. As if to add to her threat, she then threw her head back and a metallic roar filled the air.

I can only think that we had been missed by the questing eyes of the ghouls, as now they completely stopped. They were clearly conversing with each other. They looked up at Tugarin and then across to us, threw their heads up and yelled a horrible curse. Then they started to turn, and with much claw-waving they started going back down the slopes.

Will punched the air and yelled in triumph, reaching down to give Typos great scaly neck a hug. He began heaping praise and thanks on her. When she replied, I could almost sense a tone of joy and triumph in her tone.

'We wait, more can come' she said. 'The dead are not found.'

'Yes of course' replied Will, a little subdued by this reply.

'Now you can again see what no one else knows,' I added. 'Dragons have had such a bad press. Ignorant stories, I suppose because they are so frightening to all. As you have seen, they help us in areas of which people have no idea.'

I shifted my aching backside a little, then settled back down, grabbing Will's jacket. 'We have an equivalent in the southern hemisphere, you will meet him.'

'What do you mean? There is another, with a dragon, witnessing like us?'

'Yep' I smiled. 'I met mine years ago, one day with Typos, in fact only a bit further from home than here, I suppose. You are not unique. You meet just once whilst it is your turn.'

I can remember him going very quiet and shaking his head. 'People have no idea of this at all, have they? It's incredible how it has been kept so secret.'

'I know, it is weird. We, or rather you later, will keep this watched for man, with Typos' help' I laughingly added.

He said no more as we sat watching the weak sun go down behind the far of mountain. The light from it seemed to switch off. When it did so, the rescuers set up arc lights which threw a yellow light where they walked. Along the valley roads the occasional pair of car headlights wove, and through the hard mountain air the calls from the searchers now and then reached us as they crossed the mountain side.

We began to get cold despite the marvellous warmth from Typos' neck muscles, and I have to admit to getting bad leg cramp and dare I say it, needing a natural break.

'Typos' I thought to her, 'we need a stretch, legs are seizing up. Can we slip off a moment?'

She half turned her head back to us. 'You need to be quick. I will get down, only go to my left. Hang on to me, this ledge is not wide.'

I will not dwell on details at this point, suffice it to say that after a belaboured effort, with Typos putting her head down on the snow, the task was managed for us both. As a bonus, whilst standing by her and rummaging deep in my pocket, I found an old paper bag of very firmly stuck-together pineapple chunks. Clouting the bag on a handy rock, Will and I were soon back on board with mouthfuls of pineapple chunk bits.

We had only been snug for minutes, it seemed, when above us Tugarin let out a horrendous roar and three bright flames split the dark of the mountain. They illuminated her crouched form, poised as if read to launch down the hill.

Her necks extended forward in straight lines. I looked down into the valley darkness, and could just make out the hideous form of one of the creatures we had seen earlier.

'Again' thought Typos, and she reared up to send a penetrating blood-curdling roar into the valley. A searing jet of flame lit up the snow around us. The heat was only just bearable, and poor Will sitting in front flung his hands up to save his face. I was shielded by his body.

The fiery blast was followed by another shorter one, then a roar so intense her sides shook with the volume. This roar seemed to go on forever, although thinking back it was probably no more than a minute. Incidentally poor Will's face the next day was bright red colour and his eyebrows had been burned away.

At last the noise of the roaring dragons died away and darkness returned.

'Hold tight, we look now' thought Typos to us, and with a

stomach-churning leap up and forward we were flying again. She half glided and half flew in the dark down into the valley. Above the roads and the timbered houses with their tiny street lights, she loitered, presumably looking for the hideous creatures. A few wing beats saw her turn and work her way along a small river we could just make out winding its way along the valley floor.

'They are now gone' was all she thought to us. She turned and began flying up the mountainside. She quartered her way across from side to side, gaining possibly seven hundred feet on each pass.

We both knew where Tugarin was waiting, and once level with her Typos locked her wings and circled in front, whilst Will and I both heard dragon chatter flow between them. We were near enough on some of the passes for us to see this phenomenal creature, this three-headed force, so fierce, but thank goodness on the side of man.

After a while the beasts stopped communicating and we felt Typos' muscles begin contracting in earnest.

'We are done. All is safe, we return' she thought to us. Looking across at Tugarin, we were horrified by the cold contempt in the gaze with which all three heads fixed us.

I should say that the avalanche had been caused by rain falling on ice. It was later reported that one of the lead climbers had loosened a slab of ice which had fallen, triggering the fall. It had claimed nine climbers' lives and injured many more. Fortunately for them some climbers managed to turn off the face in time, and rescuers had to use helicopters and dogs to search these high altitude areas.

Mont Blanc massif is highly popular with walkers and climbers, but sadly each year there are many fatalities.

Her flight back was uneventful, following the same distance

chewing routine, working her way up in a straight line, then falling into a glide forward, until the ground almost claimed us.

The Channel showed up as a silvery ribbon, and soon after we crossed it we began dropping, until through the dark the wonderful sight of the field barn appeared.

'I have need now of you' Typos thought to me, and after a while, 'Wait, we go on.'

'What, right now?' I thought back as she landed gently on the wet grass.

'Yes, you are wanted' she answered as I helped Will slide off her neck. We had both seized up and he tried to jump on the spot, waving his arms.

'You are well?' thought Typos, turning her great eyes onto him.

'I am fine, just a bit stiff, you did wonderfully' he said, giving her neck a massive hug and making a rather embarrassing cooing noise. To give her credit she did not seem perturbed by this, almost, dare I say, enjoying it.

'I am wanted, it seems' I said. 'You all right finding your way back? You know where the key is, could you feed the dogs, and doss down in the spare room as usual? I have no idea how long I will be, but I'll catch up with you in the morning, don't lie awake.'

We said more cheerios as I climbed back onto Typos' neck.

'Right all set, up to you my friend.'

Then I heard the answer I had longed for.

'We go to your Freyja, she waits.'

I could not answer, not knowing what to say. Typos sprang up, and looking down over her shoulder I briefly saw Will look up before she twitched out.

This twitching was more prolonged and much more lengthy than normal. It seemed to go on forever, making me feel incredibly rough.

'We go back further than before, as far as I can, you are well?' was her only thought.

'Well... I have been better' was my rather sarcastic reply. 'What have you done, where are you going?'

She did not answer right away, and thinking intensely I was aware of another talking to her, just faintly. I resigned myself to quietly sitting and waiting. Looking down, I had just enough geography to realise that one of the east coast ports was below us, and then presumably miles and miles of cold grey North Sea.

She gained height in her usual straight line, her wing muscles powerfully contracting. I felt the force, and mercifully the warmth from her body entering my legs.

'Freyja wants to meet again, you can think of your future, all is possible. This is normal for Myrrdin. Your thanks you can do.'

'You and she have both said before' I started to think back.

'Your time is near... your next fully starts soon, on his own.'

Then that thought that I would always treasure: 'She has asked for you.'

'Yes... I know' was all I could think back.

I do remember that at the time being rather crushed by being made to realise that my days were nearly finished, and Freyja had thought of me still. However, as I will now try and explain in some sort of order, the thought of my death is not that grim for me. In fact what it would lead to is wonderful.

CHAPTER 13

FREYJA

That flight was probably the longest I had been on with Typos. I do not mind admitting that I had had enough that night. The cold seemed to get into every corner, only my legs, being in contact with her, felt remotely warm. It was virtually pitch black, with just the odd view of glassy white waves below us as she glided down before slogging back up.

Overhead, through a thin cloud layer, the half moon shone a pathetic light, and through gaps in the cloud the odd piece of starry sky could be seen. It was probably only the fact that I was increasingly hungry as well that stopped me nodding off, as for some reason I felt inordinately tired. My eyes kept shutting, and I remember Typos almost shouting a thought to me.

'You are well? I feel you sliding.'

'I'm fine' I lied in reply. 'Just tired and hungry, I have had a long day.'

'We will be there soon, it is all set.'

I peered forward into the black night, desperately trying to see something, anything, but there was nothing. She effortlessly slogged on, and try as I might I could detect no sign of exhaustion.

All her movements were in effortless harmony. I could not sense any breathlessness, and sitting as a mere passenger on her neck I felt useless.

As the night closed in on us and it grew increasingly cold, I was at last aware that we were losing height. Looking ahead, dark patches of forest began appearing, and two long fingers of water seemed to be running inland below us. I could not believe my eyes when below us a dark ribbon edged by small fires at regular intervals appeared.

'We are here' Typos thought, 'I will collect you in time, and return. You meet Freyja here. She waits.'

'Yes, but where are we, is this her home?'

'It is. She asked me to bring you, you need to be definite. Your time is soon finished.'

As she thought this to me, she began flaring out, her great wings beating slowly as we fell out of the sky. Below us on the clearing edge I was excited to see the figure of Freyja, and even from this height I could see her cats. Their backs were arched as they rubbed themselves against her legs, going in and out.

'Well done Typos thanks, you are here' I felt Freyja think to Typos. 'A big straw and rush bed awaits in a barn for you with your meat.'

'Myrrdin, you are expected. Welcome to Asgard, my country. We will go now to my home, my hall of Sessrumnir.'

With that she walked over to me, her arms outstretched, and gave me an embrace that felt so welcome and so needed.

'I cannot believe I am here, it feels, well, complete!' I said. 'I feel so happy to be here. You will not believe my torment waiting for you.'

I pushed her shoulders back to look at her properly, both of us smiling like idiots, and both then laughing and giggling. Her eyes in that light had the same burning brightness I remembered from before.

A brown gold-flecked shawl was draped over her shoulders, meeting a plain blue heavy-looking skirt. At her neck I glimpsed the sparkle of Brisingamen, the wondrous dwarf-made necklace. She caught me looking at it, blushed a bright red, and pulled her shawl around to cover it.

'Don't worry, I found out what you had to do to get it. I am not worried at all, it is history, gone.'

She looked up at my face, a questioning look in her eyes.

I paused. 'Believe me it's history, it is long done with.'

I took her shoulders again and looked back, trying to be reassuring.

'It is from a dreadful past' she said. She stopped and looked down at her feet, her face reddening.

'It really does not matter to me one bit' I stressed in a soft voice. I gently pulled her chin up so that she had to look me straight in the eye.

'It is history, gone. It does not affect me at all. We all have a past' I repeated.

She managed a half smile. 'Are you sure?'

'Positive, look at me. It does not matter at all. Come on, take me in, show me around. I am a tad tired and hungry. '

'What is 'tad'?' was her answer, which got me laughing again, and I put my arm around her waist as we set off to the track.

'Typos' she called, 'do you remember the main barn by the hall? My brother Frey waits to welcome you.'

'I do and I go' was Typos' tired response. We both turned, and with a wink, I swear, Typos twitched out.

'Come, I will show you all' she said, and with that she took my hand and started leading with a mock-pulling, half-skipping action amid much laughter.

There was enough light to see a handsome turreted house, or rather a mansion, at the end of the track. It was sitting on a wood edge with gently-sloping fields running down to it. A large lake formed one edge, lined by a few large trees and with the now risen and unshrouded moon reflected on its still surface.

'How beautiful!' I half whispered .

Smiling, she turned to me. 'This has been my home for ever, I love its peace and calm. Come on, they are waiting for us.'

I was momentarily worried. 'Do you mean your family?'

'No not today, later for them' she laughed back. She gave my shoulder a squeeze and smiled at me. 'No, my staff – is that what you say?'

'You have staff?'

'Only my helper, you will love her, very old but my help forever, and a cook who you will see tomorrow.'

I have to admit to a slight trepidation as we stepped under a massive oak lintel and through heavy oak and nail-studded front doors. The entrance hall gave into a massive timbered hall, with a large fire going at one end, set in a large stone inglenook. It was warm and softly lit, and there was a large polished table laid with two places. The floor was paved with massive flagstones covered with large rugs and in places, glistening with the flare lights mounted in the walls.

Two large hounds stirred awake and with long tails wagging

slowly, they came wandering over. Freyja bent down to cuddle each in turn. Then they turned and came over to me, their large brown eyes hinting at a welcome.

'Hello you two' I said without thinking, out of habit. Both hounds slammed their anchors on at this and turned to look at Freyja. She laughed out loud and bent to give their necks a rub.

'Yes he can' she said to them. 'But not in your tongue yet, he is special.'

The hounds, reassured, came over and gave me a typical doggie welcome, their faces showing their joy.

'Keep quiet about his surprise' she thought to them, giving me a playful look, and looking at the hounds she put one finger on her lips. They shook heads, turned to look again at me, and wandered back to crash down in front of the fire. One rolled over to let the heat cook its tummy.

From memory the food was delicate and delicious and the meal was filled with one good recollection that had me wondering even more; the simple use of a term.

The main course, if you want to call it that, was a delicious stew with juniper berries; I recognised the meat as venison. It was delicious and helped by light fluffy dumplings. After a few mouthfuls I realised that she had stopped to watch me.

'You call this venison, but some call it dewlap' she said.

This was a word that I still remembered from my first fall, as I lay drifting in and out of consciousness. Whilst I lay on the ground, I remember to this day, a deep voice telling me that a dewlap had caused my horse Caspian to fall.

I put my knife and fork down, looking at her.

'That is a word I have not heard for years. It has bad memories for me.'

She smiled back. 'You will soon meet that person again, he told me.'

'Who? Tell me what?' I implored, almost rising to my feet.

'Later, we have time. Eat now, you look tired. All will make sense tomorrow.'

She reached towards me across the table as if to touch my hand, with a smile that showed immense care. I started eating again, with her now and then catching my eyes with another smile.

The meal went on to finish with apples, deep red and so large that we had to cut them in half. Then there was a hard but delicious cheese. We chattered on for a while, sitting on a big pile of rugs in front of the fire, on to which she threw new logs. I cannot remember now what we spoke about particularly, but after a time, she prodded me lightly in the ribs and whispered in my ear.

'Come to bed now, you are finished. Typos told me you have been far.' She pulled me to my feet and led me across the hall towards an imposing flight of stone stairs.

Now some memories are private, and this account now reaches a private moment. Suffice it to say that the bed was a massive oak-framed affair with deep down-filled mattresses, covered by thick skins, under which we were soon very warm indeed. That is all I wish to say about the use of that bed.

In the morning, with the first light coming through the cracks in the window coverings, I was instantly awake. The realisation that next to me was the warmth of a sleeping Freyja was so new. At the same time I was aware of a plaintive thought, 'let me in, let me in!' This was matched by a rasping sound, like nails, on the door.

Freyja stirred at the sound, and half asleep, half laughing, she wriggled away from me. She stood rubbing her eyes and throwing her gold hair around, looking down at me.

'Shut your eyes tightly, a surprise comes' she said.

'What?' I said, then as requested I shut my eyes. I listened carefully as she padded across to the door, and heard it open. Then I heard claws on the floor and felt a large dog jump onto the bed. I quickly opened my eyes.

I cannot recall this moment without a tear forming. There on the bed alongside me was Milly, my first wolfhound. She had been through so much with me, had been so supportive. When she died I was never the same.

I was struck dumb. My wonderful hound looked at me, and I flung my arms around her. Through her rough, coarse coat I could feel her massive muscles. My hand ran down her long leg bones to her great long black claws. She was unchanged; exactly as I remembered her. She fixed me with one of her gazes, the great brown eyes telling me so many stories.

'How on earth?' was all I could mutter. Freyja ran back and climbed back into bed.

'I watched, could see what she means to you. I gave her the choice. I have one more surprise to show you, soon.' She paused, as if emphasizing, and looked hard at me.

'This is special, just for Myrrdins such as you, but limited. Also, to speak the truth, I wanted you.'

She looked seriously at me, then put her arm out of the covers to cuddle Milly around the neck.

'We are back, I am now happy' thought Milly to me, rolling on her side, her great head looking at me from only a foot away.

That phrase she had used – 'wanted you' - filled my head with thoughts. I turned to look at the high ceiling, and the torment and doubts must have shown on my face.

'What is wrong, what troubles you? Tell me now, I am worried' said Freyja. Looking at her, I was horrified to see tears forming. One coursed down her face to drop on the bed, turning instantly to gold. The moment when I had first met her years before came rushing back.

'Hey, it is nothing, but...' I paused, summoning the resolve, and looking at her I was mortified to see her sorrow.

'It is nothing, nothing has changed. I want to be here, have needed you for so long, but look...' I paused, looking at her, with a smile, trying desperately to reassure her. 'Let me explain.'

She wriggled up the bed with her head next to Milly, all three of us together.

As gently as I could, I started to explain that I was troubled by our apparent age difference. Then, after summoning a lot of strength, I explained that books had been written about her. When I mentioned this she pulled herself over and leaned on her elbows, looking at me.

'For studying history, for schools?' she asked, giving me a wide smile that showed her even and oh so white teeth.

I said that she was right, and explained that the books for students in the future spoke about a husband. Then I paused, looking at her intently and putting my hand onto her shoulder. At this she put her hand out to me as well, holding my fingers. 'Wait, you need to know from me,' she said.

It went very quiet for a moment.

'He was a Myrrdin like you, years and years back' she said. She paused, as it was apparent that the memory was hurting. 'Just like you, he came here, he needed to be here - complete. He did not return, and I searched for years. I found that before his winged horse could find him and bring him back, he had been killed, beyond her reach, in a hunting accident.'

On saying this, copious tears started falling and her shoulders shook. I was mortified, and tried to hold and support her.

'I feel the same now about you' was all she was able to stutter between sobs.

As she shook I thought over and over about the next. I had to ask, for it had tormented me not knowing.

'Look, there is one last thing I need to know' I said.

'Yes?' was the muffled answer, nearly lost in my arms.

'Well… students learn that you had two daughters, called Hnoss and Gersemi.' I paused. 'This has filled my thoughts. I realise that I have known nothing, nothing about you. It has been horrible.' I bowed my head, avoiding her eyes. 'You have, or had, children. I know really nothing about you!'

She did not say anything then, but after what seemed like ages, she looked up at me, and waited until I looked at her. Her eyes were drying, her cheeks still streaked with gold flecks. Her face broke into a smile, then a laugh grew and grew inside her.

Then came the response to beat all responses.

'I have no children yet. But we will have these two, it is written.'

She wriggled up the bed to look intently into my eyes, her look showed intention and joy.

'They will be yours and now I am so happy that history will be complete. These children will be yours as well - ours!'

'What?' was all I could answer. I was stunned, but I felt a thrill rising in me. 'How can that be? I mean how in time can that happen? It is more than weird, it is outrageous, impossible!'

This sounded like lunacy. Here I was from the present century, going back in time and having children in my old age.

I stopped talking for a while, my mind trying to understand how on earth this could be. I had got used to the fact that during my life I had been different and I had just about got my head around going back in time with Typos. But I had found myself planted in a previous time, and I felt thoroughly out of my depth.

She lifted a finger to her lips and I broke off. 'Wait. I will explain some things now, but later you will understand more. This is me, my life, different from yours.'

She now looked at me intently, and at this point Milly joined in. 'All is well, you have problem?'

'No, it is nothing, go back to sleep' said Freyja, rumpling the dog's great head. Milly looked at me, then shut her eyes.

Freyja pulled herself up onto her elbows. 'I am different from you. No, wait!' I was about to speak, but she lifted a hand up to cover my lips.

'In your terms I was born way before you, but in a way at the same time, and then taken back.' She stopped, as if allowing this to sink in. 'My family is ancient, but I was taken back to, do you say, the time to be. You are now in that time. If you join me you will be younger, but will age the same. I will not age at that rate. We are different.'

She paused, and I saw a tear forming again.

'You will go one day, but you will leave me with our daughters for my memories. This is what is written, if you wish.'

To say that I was stunned would be an understatement. I am aware that as you read this in your world of taxes, pollution, global warming, mortgages, car finance and so on, you will be wondering.

Think larger, as I did that morning. What about old age, food, health care, my teeth, money? It went on and on in my head.

In the end, the choice was easy.

We spent that morning lazily having a slow breakfast, then she showing me around her great house and introduced me to her lovely helper, a white-haired, slightly bent, elderly lady with a ready smile. We had to use Freyja as a translator, but with a final smile and hug from her that morning I knew I had been adopted for sure.

We went outside and I was straight away stunned by the chorus of birdsong. It filled the air with trilling, just as it had years ago when I was young. The air smelt of the nearby pine forest, and a gentle wind teased at our hair.

The lake seemed to vanish in the distance against the hillside. The meadow stretched far away on the other, the grass long and waving gently in the air. It seemed to run right up to the far-off mountains, whose brilliant white caps I could see the deep blue sky.

All was quiet apart from some far-off choughs squabbling over something in the grass, and overhead the broad wings of a big raptor, possibly a sea eagle, glided.

We walked down and around the lakeside, where a few waterfowl swam, coming over in hope of getting some treats from us. Milly roamed ahead of us, periodically looking back to check that we were following. 'You are not going again?' was all she had said.

'Daft dog' I said to Freyja. 'As if I could.'

We had got beyond the lake when Freyja stopped walking, put her hands on my shoulders and looked me straight in the eye. A smile lifted the corners of her lips.

'It is now. I have one last present for you, one last to show my thoughts, my plans, just for you.'

I was about to say 'what do you mean?' when she put her hands on my waist and turned me around.

'Look to that corner of the meadow and watch. Do nothing else, just watch. One last gift for you, to show my resolve. Milly, now if you will.'

Milly turned to look at her, and I swear smiled. Then she turned to race off like an arrow for the far corner.

'What on earth have you arranged?' I asked, turning to look at her.

'He has been waiting. You will see soon, be patient,' she said back, laughing and twisting away to escape from my mock grab at her.

'Wait' she said again, turning to look down the meadow. I turned, wondering what was going to happen. The clouds up above gently went over, the air was warm and the gentle breeze still gently tugged.

After a moment I thought I heard hooves, a horse at a canter, somewhere out of sight, and then Milly's excited barking. On the far horizon a horse appeared, and as it got nearer I saw that it was a dark bay with a white star. A voice from my childhood was shouting all sort of excited babble.

I turned to Freyja, stunned.

'What have you done, you marvellous thing? It cannot be! It's Caspian!'

I turned her to me and embraced her as if my life was going.

'Yes, it is, his spirit. He meant so much to you. He is here, that is all I can do.' She paused. 'It was he you heard talking of the dewlaps.'

We both turned and held hands as we watched the pair of them arrive. I do not mind admitting that I trembled a little, my excitement betraying me.

Caspian was exactly as I remembered and as he arrived, he came to a great sliding stop that peeled a bit of turf off. We touched noses and shared our breath. You need to be horsy to appreciate the complete joy of this.

'It has been long' he thought to us, 'too long, but never apart again.'

The reunion - what a hopeless term - took maybe an hour. There was a lot of catching up to do. Freyja stood watching at a distance, hands on hips, with a smile that seemed to split her face, just watching and waiting.

'Go on then, off you go you three,' she said finally.

'What do you mean?' I answered.

'Caspian knows' was her answer, with a mischievous smile.

As she said this Caspian bent his front legs and then tucked them back under and lay down. 'On we go' he thought to me, almost ordering me.

'Go on you three, have fun, I will wander back and think of food for us, be safe,' said Freyja. With that she turned and started walking off.

'Caspian, I am not as agile as I was' I pointed out.

'Neither am I' was his simple answer. That was why he had lain down to make it easier. However, with a lot of leg pulling by me, I wound my hands in his mane and he got awkwardly to his feet. Then he shook like a dog, shifting water and getting everything in place. I know you are thinking, what about a saddle and bridle? Well, I did not need them, I was snug and safe riding him bareback. It felt just perfect to be back on him, so much so that I do not mind admitting to you that I became a little emotional. But those feelings passed as the joy of trotting along once again with a wolfhound ranging either side filled every pore of my being. I was taken back to how it had all begun, riding my father's horse over the Dorset hills, travelling for miles. I did not remember the fall, only the time in hospital afterwards.

Through it all came my thoughts of Jules, the Merlin I replaced. How my hospitalisation had nearly wrecked his plan, my first dragon flight, and my second spell in hospital after Shola was ambushed and killed by the Wind Furies.

The morning passed in a series of mental exchanges between us as we crossed the grassy swards, and then at last the hall came back in sight. Caspian stopped, and with a bit of manoeuvring I slid off.

'I will be back for good soon, you will see, be safe until then' I thought to him.

'Good, we are all complete again' he replied, and with that he turned to walk off.

He stopped to turn and look at us after a few yards, to rear, buck and finally go galloping off, so glad to be alive. I turned to Milly, who lifted her head to look at me.

'Right come on then, I am hungry, and I nearly said I could eat a horse!'

With many chuckles between us and lots of joshing, mock growling and wrestling, we went in to find Freyja.

* * *

All too soon, as Freyja and I stood arm in arm by the lakeside the next morning, a call from Typos arrived. As I turned to Freyja, about to tell her, she lifted her eyes to look straight at me.

'I know. She comes to take you back... for now, but only until you return.'

She suddenly looked worried and half ran to throw her arms around me. 'You will return?'

'How could I not?' was my answer.

As I said this my lovable great lump of a dragon appeared by us. Her lemony smell filled the air, her coat glistening with beads of sweat. I really did not want to go or say goodbye, and was mortified to have to.

'I will be back soon, don't worry' I said and then, meeting her eye, 'Our daughters are the future, I will be back with Typos.'

I gave her a hug and a final kiss and then, as she turned, began getting onto my usual spot on Typos. Wriggling into position on her neck, I looked across to Freyja to see that she was unashamedly crying. The golden droplets coursed down her face, with a few already glistening like gold at her feet.

'Until next time, when I return' I called, feeling my own voice waver, and lifting a hand. She looked so sad, but she did manage to smile. She lifted a hand in a half wave, and Typos stretched out her wings and jumped into the air.

'We go back to your now' Typos thought to me. She did not fly off straight away but circled, allowing me to look down and carry on waving to a watching Freyja. When she was a much smaller figure, Typos turned towards the weak sun and headed out to the distant sea.

'You are fine' she thought to me.

I was not really able to think straight and give her an answer, and after a pause I heard from her again. 'What do you want, to return to your time with the last Myrrdin? He started you. Do you want to return to her? Or something else I can do? You do not have many days.'

Now that I was leaving Freyja I hated it, but nudging in my mind... well, to be honest it seemed amazing. I was for once undecided. At a loss. The whole concept seemed at the time something I wanted, yet so bizarre.

'I will need to think, Typos, I am at a loss' I replied.

'You have until the night of your birthday, then you call and it is done. Your time is nearly over. The new Myrddin is ready. His time is soon, as yours finishes.'

The flight back seemed to take somehow longer than going, and thought conversation was limited. Looking up, the constellations twinkled in a clear sky. The pole star dominated my thoughts and I was reassured in a way to be able to work out our direction.

Soon the coast appeared, and I felt my spirits lighten a little. Looking down, the lights of motorway traffic showed as a red stream on one side, almost nose to tailing in their slow progress. On the other side was a corresponding stream of white approaching headlights.

This marvellous, wonderful creature then stunned me.

'Whilst there is peace I will say that you have been my first, and if all that follow are the same I will be happy. My mother found you the same.'

Now how could I answer that?

'Thank you Typos, you are and have been a privilege' I said. As I said this I gave her neck a vigorous rub and was surprised to feel a tremor go through her.

'We could meet again many times, I can go back and meet. You will be in my reach for long, that is until you go on' she said.

I was stunned by this reply and it took me a while to get my head around it. Of course, back in that time with Freyja I would be alive and so Typos could meet me, wolfhound, horse and her. It was getting easier.

As I looked down in the dark, the lights of the motorway gave me a good indication of our progress. As if following a map, she turned towards the soft outlines of the Dorset hills.

'It is dark, we are not seen. The next Myrrdin waits for you. We go into your home paddocks.'

'Fine' I thought back and then, 'Hey, I have just thought – Typos, along the river at home a power line runs, be careful for goodness sake!'

'That is fine, I know of it' was her rather short response.

'It is just that I thought of it' I answered back, having no wish to replay that frightful night when her mother had been killed on the other side of the village.

She did not answer, and as she twitched out I was intrigued to see a view of the house I had never seen before. It may seem hard to believe, but in all the years of flying with her, I had never flown over the back of the house and the home paddock.

The ground seemed to rush up as Typos flared onto the ground, and waiting under a large beech tree I saw Will. In the half-light he looked across, lifting a hand in welcome.

'You will call on your birthday night, and I will if I need you before' thought Typos as I wriggled down to the ground.

'Of course my friend, go carefully' I thought back, giving her neck the usual hug and breathing in her characteristic smell.

'I go' was all she answered, and she went just like that.

'Hello Will, you all right?' I called out, pulling my shirt back in and jumper straight.

'Yes fine, all sheep, dogs and horses present and correct. I have cooked some grub for us. A surprise eh! Hope that's all right.' He looked across at me. 'Been far? You have been gone two days, I was getting a bit anxious.'

I smiled at him. 'One day it will be all yours to worry about!'

The pair of us started walking across the orchard, to be met by my tail-wagging old Labrador and the wriggling terriers.

'My birthday next week, on Thursday' I said. 'Going to have a bit of supper for a few chums, you can make it surely?'

He looked across at me, cuddling all the dogs in one tail-wagging churning heap at his feet.

'Of course, try and keep me away, I'm always hungry.'

We went in to enjoy his supper, which incidentally was not half bad.

CHAPTER 14

A CHILD'S TALE

I awoke very early the next day, after a night, if I am truthful, mainly spent lying awake. After a big mug of coffee and sharing a packet of digestive biscuits with an ancient Labrador and two begging Jack Russells, I left the house. The early morning was so dark that could still have been night. It was overcast, with scudding clouds, and very little sunlight.

The village was quiet with only a milkman to meet us on the far side as we walked down through the orchard and over the river bridge. The river was running only a few inches deep in places, unusual for the winter. From the bridge I was able to watch a trout finning on the edge of a deeper section. Catching my movement, it suddenly shot deeper and had gone.

Further down, the river crossed gravel beds, and here a moorhen strutted about, its head bobbing in time with its strides as it darted down to peck at the odd piece of weed.

I stayed there for about half an hour, with the dogs patiently waiting for us to move up and tackle the hill out of the village. I moved in and lifted a hand in acknowledgement to the paper man who drives into the village. He waved back as out of custom I patted my thigh, signalling to the dogs we were off.

'Not too fast, and keep in you lot' I thought to them.

'Don't worry, we will be on the edge until the hill, that is if we are going that far?'

'We will see. No hurry, I just want to look down on it all again.'

I am not going to labour the point, but suffice it to say that in my younger days I could and did run up here. Not today though, just a gentle stroll with a few stops, moving in once for a car was about the measure of it.

Half way up we stopped and I turned to take in the view of the village below and my own hill on the far side. I could just make out the barn where so many times I had called Shola and then Typos.

Hidden just below me, with just its roof visible, was the barn Jules had lived in. Here my time as Myrrdin had been explained to me, and I had begun all those years before. Sadly it had not been lived in since his death and had been left to return to the earth, decaying and rotting. It had left its footprint in the form of piles of stones where the walls had been.

The yard that it stood in had a new farm with open-fronted buildings, so maybe one day some enterprising person would rebuild it. Maybe they would wonder what that site had witnessed in the past. Unless my first account is found, they would never know.

I smiled at the thought of that and with a final look at the rookery, with rooks beginning to 'smokestack' above, I turned and carried on up to the main road. This has changed too in all the years, getting busier. I waited for a gap in the traffic to allow us all to cross.

The hill here is fairly steep, with the grass kept short by the sheep. The track winds a way up past clumps of brambles, a few lumps of rock sticking out, and a few wind-pruned hawthorn bushes. On the side a few beech trees and further around ancient oaks manage to stand against the winds.

This morning the woolly bunch just lifted their heads to try to work us out. They must have been happy enough resuming their cropping, one or two staying with heads up watching.

'Go on you lot' I said to the dogs. 'Give those woollies room, but off you go, explore!'

The dogs charged off, but India soon gave it up as a bad job. She stopped to sniff her way along, just now and then turning to look at where I had got to.

As I headed slightly across the hill rather than up, the sea in the bay came into sight, and with the wind coming off it it smelt heavenly, salty and fresh. I stopped to take in the view that had held me entranced for years. The sea looked a dull grey, with white horses showing, and very far out three largish boats, possibly one a tanker, worked along the coast.

Looking down towards the hills of Pilsdon and Lewesdon, then back inland to Beaminster Down, the view stopped all thought, as it always has, and I found myself lost in the view. Down below me was the patch of hill where my first accident with Caspian had happened, as a young man at the start of it all. Of course the actual accident has gone from my memory, but I still remember being in the hospital, and of course the ghastly second time with Shola's death.

At the thought of it all, I shuddered, and although there was really no need I pulled my jacket collar up, whistled up the dogs and started down. I reached the level and chuckled out aloud to myself at the first memory of Jules calling Shola to him, thinking how petrified I had been on that very spot. Now, after years and years of being with dragons, it seems normal, but I bet reading this account you cannot believe it.

We all wandered back down. The village was waking up, and thin trails of blue wood smoke were emerging from some of the chimneys.

The dogs were fed, chickens let out and the few lambs left in the home paddock checked, and then my own breakfast called. The frying pan has always started my day and that morning the eggs had just started chattering and going crispy brown on the edges when in the yard, the throb of Will's new bike announced his arrival.

I looked up through the kitchen window, lifting a hand and then reached down two more eggs from the shelf. I had no need to ask, as he was always hungry and growing like a weed. He must have grown a foot since I had introduced Typos to him.

'Hey, morning, you all right?' was his first comment as he opened the door to be greeted by an avalanche of ecstatic dogs.

'Yes, really good, we have all had an early stretch. I've chucked a couple of eggs on for you. Here, do something useful, get the coffee going.' I smiled across at him.

'Yes sure, but I have got a surprise, well, a birthday treat for you. I know it's a bit early.'

I looked quizzically at him. 'What have you done, you menace?' I joked, passing him a plate of eggs and toast.

'Well it's not just me, it's your birthday in a few days.' He stopped, smiling at me. 'You're being picked up in an hour and taken up to see the last few drives of the morning on the main shoot. No, wait,' he put a hand up. 'We know long distance walking over mud and rubbish isn't really for you, so you're being picked up in the keeper's four wheel drive, so there!' he grinned. 'Also, you're having a special picnic in the beaters' hut, before they bring you back.'

He stopped, looking at my stunned face.

'That's brilliant! Really kind and unexpected. Lovely!'

'Not at all. They all wanted to, you had shot for years and the last few years you've missed, so this makes it possible. Most of them will be with you for nosh on the actual day, so there, job done.'

He laughed. I just had time to clean my teeth and change into smarter clothes and pull my waxy on. Outside, the keeper's pickup arrived right on cue. I was being driven by the underkeeper, who gave me a big grin as he leaned over to open the door, the outside catch being broken. Two pickers-up were sitting happily in the back and looking through the window above their heads, the back was full of grinning Labradors and a spaniel. They were all wagging tails fit to burst and trying to look out.

'This is so unexpected, it's a real treat' I said as I pulled one leg in to get comfortable, then shut the door.

'Hey not at all, we all wanted to. We haven't seen you for a while. If you stay with this wagon, we can go from one drive to the next without you having any aggro.'

The drive up the hill, out of the village and then up to the shoot was full of, shall I say, man chat. I will not elaborate, but you know the somewhat racy humour that young men fire out when they're together. Guns, beaters and pickers-up always met in the school yard, and the amount of birthday wishes got me a little embarrassed.

Soon the day began with the shoot captain giving normal briefings and commands, and with peg numbers drawn we all moved off. As usual the beaters went off in their tractor-drawn trailer, guns walking to the first drive with pickers-up and keen Labradors already looking around, as if expecting that their work had already begun. I stayed in the pickup, following on and passing around the first of the almost compulsory sweets.

Before lunch that day there were three drives, some birds shot and many missed. When the whistles signalled the drive's end, the dogs went to work. Two of the guns had us watching them most, as their shooting appearing effortless; the birds were all being killed with one shot, never double tapped, although they always chose the more demanding higher bird. The back of the pickup was soon loaded with birds, hung in pairs, and we moved on from one vantage point behind the line to another.

I am bothering to mention this day for two personal reasons, apart from it being a lovely full day. First, the last-but-one morning drive saw us heading down to the long valley where every spring I saw the Beltane ritual. I must have gone quiet, lost in my thoughts.

'You all right sir?' the underkeeper asked.

'Yes fine don't worry, just thinking back to memories. It's years since I was here' I lied, looking across at him.

'Well it is a bit wild here' he answered, wrestling with the steering and putting the gears into low ratio. 'Nice though, so peaceful.'

The line of guns was across the valley floor and from the car parked on the valley side I could look down. Although the shooting was thorough, my mind wandered off, to remember the lady as she walked along broadcasting, the bell music and her animal 'forwarders' making sure it was safe for her. I had reconciled my mind that spring to the idea of never seeing her again.

I must have smiled at the thought of what they did not know, those chaps there that morning. How it would all be unknown to them.

'Go on, tell me what you're laughing at, must be something good, go on' said the underkeeper.

'Oh, nothing at all, just a few memories that is all. Don't they shoot well?' I changed the subject and met his query with a smile.

Before the afternoon began we had all arranged to meet in the beaters' hut for lunch as normal. Flasks of soup, coffee, pies and sandwiches filled hungry mouths. No speeches were made, thankfully, but one of the pickers-up, a man I knew well, kindly started a 'happy birthday', and a very good bottle of sloe gin was put to good use.

Now I can tell you about the second part, much more in my memory. While we all sat down, a few children of the beaters and pickers-up whizzed about outside, laughing and having one of those chasing games. They hurtled about, stopping now and then to raid lunch boxes. I have to say that most that day seemed to be stuffing mainly chocolate.

It did become obvious after a while that one little girl, probably about seven, was not running about. She sat on her mother's lap, looking wide-eyed and saying little. She had long blonde hair falling down, just hiding her blue eyes. Her smile showed a few gaps were teeth had fallen out, and her head stuck out of a big jumper that said it belonged to a well-known bear. Her skinny legs swung to and fro, ending in great big boots which showed a mock fur lining.

I leaned over, offering her and her mum one of my pineapple sweets.

'Here you go, try one of these. Had a good morning? What you thinking about?'

The lass looked at me with wide eyes, then up at her mother.

'Thank you, they look lovely, go on Ellie, have one and say thank you.'

The lass helped herself, politely thanking me, and soon all three mouths started enjoying the sweets.

'She is an imaginative little girl, everything happening' smiled her mother at me, then down at Ellie. 'Bit distracted today, aren't you?'

'But it's true, I don't fib, I can see special things you know' retorted Ellie, almost jumping up in her seat.

'I am sure you can, you're clever. What you seen then Ellie? No go on, let me guess – fairies? Pixies? You know they are real, I've seen em too' I said bending down to her level. I looked up at her mother, then across at Ellie.

Then the remark that hit me. 'She saw a dragon three nights ago, didn't you Ellie? Go on, tell the man.'

I really did not know what to say. 'No! Did you? Well if it makes you feel better I know they're real, I think I saw one too. Go on, when, what were you doing?'

I looked at her mum, who smiled back, giving me a surreptitious wink.

'Go on tell him, I'm sure it is true' she said. 'Everything else you say is.'

Ellie looked at me, then as her confidence grew, started speaking quicker, more loudly and with great excitement. She pushed herself to the edge of her seat, with her mother looking down quietly and holding her shoulder for support. As she remembered her story, she began to throw her arms about.

She had been tucked up in bed, with the curtains pulled back, gazing from her pillow at the starry sky. When she was almost on the point of dropping off she had become instantly awake, and in horror she had tried to call for her mother, but her voice for some reason, she said, had not wanted to work. Grabbing her bear by its arm, she had gone over to the window to peep out, keeping herself half hidden by the curtain.

She stopped at this point and looked up at her mum.

'Go on tell him what you saw then,' she said.

'I saw a dragon, really big, flying in, with a man or something sitting on his back, on its neck.'

I was stunned by this and looked up her mother, who fixed me with a look, meaning 'get out of that then'.

'Well Ellie, I don't what to say or think about that' I said.

'It was not making any fire or anything like that, no noise I could hear. It was all black with great big wings. It was massive and it had big dangling legs.'

Some rapid thinking on my feet.

'You know years ago I read about this. No reason at all to doubt you…'

I stopped, looking up at her mum, who lifted an eyebrow at me.

'You know I think you're really lucky, a privileged person. How many people in the whole world could say that? I'm older than your mum and I have seen strange things, but never a dragon.' I have to admit that at this point I wished the truth could be told. 'No one really knows, crikey in the years ahead who knows what will be seen. People will say remember that girl, Ellie, didn't she see one? You'll be famous, who knows? Anyway, did you see it for long? What happened?'

She jumped to her feet and fixed me with a penetrating gaze.

'I saw it go down, actually it must have landed near you.' She stopped, turning to her mother again, then back. 'Don't you live near the river?'

'Well yes, somewhere near there, perhaps that was the night my dogs barked like crazy.'

'I didn't see it after that, but you believe me, don't you?'

'Yes Ellie, I have no problem believing you. You carry on looking. Well done, and thank you for telling me. You have been very lucky.' I looked at her with a serious face. 'Very lucky indeed. I'm jealous, Bet your mum is really impressed! I'm sure dragons are real, I don't think we need to be frightened of them, in fact I believe they're probably here to help us. Well done.'

Ellie sat back down, looked up at her mother, then stood up and bounced outside.

'Well, what a story' she said. 'She'll be a writer when she's older that one, totally exhausting at times. Thank you for putting up with her, really kind, gave her a bit of confidence.'

'Well she has a great imagination for sure, kids see strange things at times. Any way she is lovely. She's a credit to you.'

I stayed for the best part of the afternoon, and was dropped off back at home clutching a brace of pheasants.

* * *

Now I have to tell you that I have sneaked off for a moment to finish these memories for you. The noise from my chums down below percolates up the stairs as my birthday nosh has moved on to the coffee and nightcap stage, so I have a couple of hours left.

I think these accounts might help you get some sense out of what you see, and who knows, in the future when more is discovered and known, it might all make sense.

I am happy that Will is carrying on this position. It is safe, doing a bit to ensure your safety from forces you can only guess at and keeping natural forces honoured and respected.

As for me, I have decided that tonight when Typos calls I will ask her to reunite my spirit with Freyja, Milly and Caspian, but I am going to ask if India can join us.

I will leave this now and sneak out to bury these notes under the log pile in the old stable for someone - who knows who? - to find, one day.

* * *

Spindle the old buzzard was watching the house one morning when the frost was so thick he had heard it almost snapping on the grass. From his vantage point in the old beech on the hillside he had seen cars, including a couple of big black ones, arrive and cruise slowly up the hill.

Later he went soaring across the village, his old eyes trying to focus down on the small party of humans standing around a hole dug in the ground. At this point his airspace had been threatened by a gaggle of noisy rooks from the village edge. Soon they had realised what had happened and made a dive back to the rookery. The noise of crying, yelling, bawling rooks filled the air.

A woman hanging out her washing in the cold air looked across, thinking the rooks must be reacting to an intruder, a fox or something. She was not to know that they had started their ancient lamentation chorus.

From his aerial vantage, Spindle glided over to see the people moving off.

The next morning his sharp eyes spotted the new Myrrdin he was following now leave the house with a black Labrador in tow. The pair went up the hill, and as usual man and dog parted company at the field gate. The lab sat down, tail twitching slowly, resigned to wait.

Spindle took off briefly, shifting his vantage point to the remains of an old elm standing in the hedge. Settling, he roused his feathers to make himself appear twice as big as usual, shook and then settled down, gripping the branch to watch.

The man went into the barn, and after looking around and acknowledging Spindle with a look, he knelt on the ground.

As Spindle had expected, after a few moments the air horse appeared. Spindle watched as the man got up and gave the great beast a welcoming hug before springing on.

In a second they had gone, and Spindle settled down to wait, as usual.

* 9 7 8 1 8 6 1 5 1 2 8 9 5 *

ND - #0496 - 270225 - C0 - 229/152/17 - PB - 9781861512895 - Matt Lamination